PETER SCHLEMIEL

PETER SCHLEMIEL

the man who sold his shadow

Adelbert von Chamisso

Translated from the German
and with an Introduction
by Peter Wortsman

Illustrated by Harold Wortsman

Fromm International
Publishing Corporation

Published in 1993 by Fromm International
Publishing Corporation, New York

Originally published in German as
Peter Schlemihls wundersame Geschichte in 1814

MANUFACTURED IN THE UNITED STATES OF AMERICA
Printed on acid-free, recycled paper
First U.S. edition

Library of Congress Cataloging-in-Publication Data
Chamisso, Adelbert von, 1781-1838
[Peter Schlemihls wundersame Geschichte. English]
Peter Schlemiel: the man who sold his shadow / Adelbert von Chamisso;
translated and with an introduction by Peter Wortsman. —1st U.S. ed.
p. cm.
ISBN 0-88064-142-8 (acid-free paper)
I.Title
PT1834.P6E5 1993
833'.6—dc20 93-2832 CIP

CONTENTS

ILLUSTRATIONS

The Displaced Person's Guide to Nowhere

It is an overstated truism, perhaps—though, like most truisms, for the most part true—that the two key prerequisites of the literary pursuit are a sense of place and a command of the native idiom. Like the Faulkner of Yoknapatawpha County or the Marquez of Macondo, writers worth their salt are generally supposed to be astute homeboys, local yokels with a canny ear for backyard palaver and a keen eye for the contour of the land. Certain notable exceptions, however, wreak havoc with the rule. A formidable literary "foreign legion" comprising uprooted aristocrats and paupers, seafarers, adventurers, itinerant intellectuals, and refugees of every ilk have hip-hopped across linguistic and geopolitical borders, and in the process, have created a parallel tradition to the literature of place—call it the literature of displacement.

For reasons that run the gamut from personal to political, these "lingoverts"—a term I am herewith coining to connote the internal psychic and emotional transformations that accompany linguistic conversion—took exile to the limit, shedding not only the outward trappings of national affiliation, but also that most intimate ID: the very syllables of self.

English literature has been immeasurably enriched by the vision and voice of such great lingoverts as the Polish count turned seafarer, Jozef Korzeniowski (alias Joseph Conrad); the Danish baroness turned coffee planter, Karen Blixen (alias Isaak Dinesen); and the uprooted Russian noble butterfly collector,

Vladimir Nabokov. The French have profited from the political and social upheavals of modern times and the lure of a nation in love with its language by welcoming the diverse talents of: Dutchman J. K. Huysmans; Irishman Samuel Beckett; Rumanian Eugene Ionesco; Catalonian Fernando Arrabal; and American Julian Green—to mention only the most famous examples.

German literature too has garnered its share of the spoils. Within the confines of the two great modern German empires, Prussia and Austro-Hungary, shifting borders and political alliances fostered a state of linguistic flux and a tendency on the part of threatened minorities seeking at least an illusion of security to huddle under the protective umbrella of German language and culture. So the Jews of Czechoslovakia scorned the Hebrew of their scholars, the Yiddish of their grandparents, and the Czech of their immediate neighbors, opting for the dominant lingua franca. (Franz Kafka, though not a lingovert, strictly speaking, is nonetheless a product of the process.) German letters forfeited the quatrilingual Nobel Laureate, S. Y. Agnon (born in Galicia, then part of Austro-Hungary) to modern Hebrew. Ironically, though, one of the great German poets of modern time, Paul Celan, a border Jew from Bukovina, who spoke Rumanian, Russian, Hebrew, or Yiddish, depending on the context, composed his harrowing lyric lament to the victims of Nazi atrocities in the language of Goethe.

It should come as little surprise, then, given the many enigmas of literary history, that one of the most haunting expressions of the German Romantic spirit, perhaps the ultimate poetic portrayal of displacement, *Peter Schlemiel,* drew its name and inspiration from a Jewish notion and was written by a Frenchman.

Louis Charles Adelaïde de Chamisso de Boncourt (better known as Adelbert von Chamisso), born in 1781 on his family's estate, Château Boncourt, in the Champagne, fled the French Reign of Terror with his aristocrat parents in 1790 and, following a circuitous escape route, eventually ended up in Berlin. There he attended the Französisches Gymnasium and proceeded under the patronage of the Emperor Friedrich Wilhelm II (whose wife he served as a page) to enter a military academy, and thereafter to join the Prussian army. When, in 1801, First Consul Napoleon Buonaparte declared an amnesty, calling on all exiled aristocrats to return home, Chamisso's parents responded to the call, leaving behind their young son, now a Prussian officer, to hold the fort in the eventuality of a possible retreat. A series of unfortunate events, including the untimely death of his parents and the declaration of war between France and Prussia, made Chamisso's situation all the more precarious, particularly following a decree issued by Napoleon in 1806, whereby any Frenchman found in foreign military service was to be executed within twenty-four hours of his capture.

Caught between two countries and two cultures, inhabiting a kind of psychic no-man's-land, Chamisso was faced with a terrible conflict that grew to encompass every aspect of his young life, a conflict that moreover led to an early suicide attempt. He put it this way in a letter he wrote in German to a friend:

> I just don't know how to braid the wreath—I can and cannot whip the disparate strands into any semblance of peace and harmony . . . religion; honor; the great duel; laws; the ideal and the reality; fatherland; solitary wrestling with my fate; faith as if in a fable; the spirit of God does not waft over the waters; America and Europe; Asia the cradle; blacks and whites; French Revolution the prelude, a new dawning; Germanness; Frenchness; Luther; Pope; Catholic; humanity; fate . . .

He expressed similar sentiments in French in a letter to the illustrious Madame de Staël (the one-woman cultural bridge and clearinghouse between Germany and France), whose acquaintance he had made as a result of his collaboration in the French translation of several lectures by the German philosopher, Friedrich Schlegel:

> I am a Frenchman in Germany and a German in France; a Catholic among the Protestants, Protestant among the Catholics; a philosopher among the religious . . . , a mundane among the savants, and a pedant to the mundane; Jacobin among the aristocrats, and to the democrats a nobleman, a man of the Ancien Regime . . . Nowhere am I at home . . . !

The pressures of such psychic turmoil and the painful reality of his status as an enemy alien proved untenable—particularly for a Prussian officer. Something had to give. Though a soldier by training, Chamisso was a scholar and poet at heart, and loathed the crude rituals and rigors of the military life. His feeling of awkwardness continued to express itself for years in nightmares in which he appeared on parade having forgotten his sword. (What would Freud have made of this?) One day, as he recalled in a letter, he "shot up out of sleep and wiped away the tears rolling down my cheeks . . . For me in this century," he realized, "no sword will do, the quill is my only refuge."

Aside from a flourishing correspondence, his literary output up until that point had been unremarkable, if promising. He was still in the process of what he described as a "tireless wrestling with the language"—that language being German. "Il faudra que j'écrive quelque chose en allemand; car au fait il faudra bien apprendre cette coquine de langue" ("I really ought to write something in German, since, after all, I do have to learn this minx of a language"), he had confessed to a friend at the Französisches Gymnasium in Berlin some years before. Now, as a lieutenant in the Prussian army, a mastery of German became an absolute imperative. His painstakingly acquired German, however inspired, would forever be marked by mistakes (corrected for publication by his friend and publisher, Julius Eduard Hitzig) and curious turns of phrase that lent his syntax a special charm. And though he continued to count in French and, it is said, muttered French on his deathbed, with a fierce determination Chamisso adopted German as his adult literary and scholarly tongue.

Later in life, in the introduction to his popular *Journey Around the World,* (an account of a Russian-led expedition to Antarctica in which, as a naturalist of note, he participated), Chamisso reflected back on the circumstances surrounding the creation of the tale that was to make his name a household word:

> The world events of the year 1813, in which I was not able to take an active part—for I had forfeited a fatherland, or rather had not yet adopted one—tore me apart repeatedly without deflecting me from my chosen path. That summer, to distract myself and to amuse the children of a friend, I wrote the fairy tale, *Peter Schlemiel.*

The "world events" of which he speaks followed the fall of Hameln (where his regiment was based) to the French, the Prussian capitulation, his own long-awaited discharge from the army, several ill-fated trips to France, and finally, an attempt to reestablish a semblance of normalcy for himself in Germany, as an enemy alien in his adoptive home.

As an outsider and the butt of considerable xenophobic sentiment, Chamisso gravitated naturally to the orbit of that other popular target of public displeasure, the Jews. In Berlin, he frequented the famous literary salons of Henriette Herz and Rahel Levin (who would later marry one of his closest friends, Karl August Varnhagen von Ense). Hitzig was a converted Jew, as were many of Chamisso's other friends and associates. It was, as Hannah Arendt points out in *Rahel Varnhagen: The Life of a Jewish Woman,* a period of great social ferment, marked by the rise of the bourgeoisie and the waning of aristocratic power; and outcasts, intellectuals, and oddballs from all quarters assembled in the living rooms of the ultimate outcast. Here Chamisso found a safe haven, and came ineluctably to identify with the Christian medieval archetype of the "Wandering Jew" and the Jewish notion of the hapless "schlemiel."

In a letter to his brother, who proposed a French translation of *Peter Schlemiel,* Chamisso specified that the hero's name must under no circumstances be changed. "Schlemihl, or rather Schlemiel, is a Hebrew name," he wrote,

> and means Gottlieb, Theophil or Beloved of God. This, in the everyday parlance of the Jews, is their designation for clumsy or unlucky souls who succeed at nothing in this world. A Schlemiel breaks his finger in his vest pocket or falls on his back and breaks his nose.

With a touch of the self-deprecating humor inherited from his friends, the young Chamisso undoubtedly saw himself as a blundering schlemiel.

When, in 1813, war once again broke out between Prussia and France, Hitzig counseled Chamisso to lie low for a while, and arranged for him to make use of his botanical skills tending the gardens of the Count von Itzenplitz in Kunersdorf. It was here, in the summer months of 1813, that he composed *Peter Schlemiel* to pass the time and entertain Hitzig's children.

Certain texts errupt as naked emanations of the soul, bursts of pain transmuted directly into poetry. Such is the case with Kafka's "Metamorphosis," the ultimate black comedy of bugging-out: "As Gregor Samsa awoke one morning from uneasy dreams he found himself transformed in his bed into a gigantic insect." And such is the case with Samsa's spiritual precursor, "Peter Schlemiel," the marginal man with literally no place under the sun. Though both were German classics, it is clearly no coincidence that the former was written in 1912 (virtually on the eve of World War I) by a Czech Jew caught in the culture shock of a crumbling Austro-Hungarian Empire, and the latter almost a century earlier by a French nobleman eluding the clashing furies of his former compatriots and his adoptive countrymen.

Both tales struck their creators as bolts of literary lightning hurled by the thunderstorm of history and filtered through the imagistic firmament of the unconscious. Both elicit in the reader an embarrassed burst of Bergsonian laughter, a socially corrective chortle all too cognizant of the subliminal implications of being reduced to a bug and of forfeiting the virile bulge of a shadow. Kafka howled hilariously, in the precise bureaucratic German of his social circumstance. Chamisso, hiding out from a world in which one facet of his identity was at war with the other, might well have opted for suicide. Fortunately for himself and for posterity, he reached for the pen. Having turned himself inside out and tapped into the very core of his terror, he proceeded with German syntax and French esprit to tell the consummate Jewish joke.

Did you hear the one about the man who sold his shadow to enhance his social standing? No? Well then, read on!

— *P.W.*

PETER SCHLEMIEL

–1–

Following a fortuitous if less than pleasant voyage, we finally pulled into port. As soon as the dinghy dropped me ashore, I hoisted my meager baggage onto my back, and pressing my way through the teeming multitudes of that harbor town, I stopped at the first flophouse whose shabby shingle caught my eye. When I asked for a room, the houseboy gave me one look and immediately led me up to the garret. I had them bring me water to wash up and thereafter requested precise directions to the home of Mr. Thomas John.

"Take the North Gate, and it's the first manor on your right, a big, new structure of red and white marble with many columns. Can't miss it."

"Thanks," I said. It was still quite early in the day. I untied my miserable bundle, pulled out my realtered black frock coat, donned my best dress clothes, slipped the letter of introduction into my breast pocket, and set off immediately to meet the man who, I hoped, would help me in my modest plans at self-improvement.

After hiking up the long northern road and reaching the city gate, I soon spotted the marble columns shimmering through the verdure. "Here I am," I thought. I wiped the dust off my shoes with my handkerchief, straightened my tie, and murmuring a prayer to God, rang the doorbell. The door sprang open. There on the threshold I was obliged to undergo an interrogation; at last the doorman announced my arrival, and I had the honor of being shepherded into the gardens, where Mr. John was just then entertaining a small party of guests. I immediately recognized the man by the shimmer of his impeccable self-satisfaction. He received me quite nobly—as a rich man receives a poor devil; he even deigned to face me without turning away from the others, and took the letter of introduction out of my hand.

"Well, well! From my brother, is it; haven't heard head nor tail of him in years. He's well, I trust?—wherever he is," he continued, rejoining his guests without waiting for an answer, and motioned with the letter for me to tag along to the top of the hill—"That's where I plan to have them put up the new building." He broke open the seal without even interrupting his conversation with the others, the subject of which was wealth. "Frankly," he maintained, "anyone who isn't worth at least a million is nothing but—if you'll forgive the term—a sniveling worm."

"How true, how true!" I cried out in full accord, with a fulsome, oozing enthusiasm.

This must have pleased him, for he smiled at me and said, "Stick around, my friend, later perhaps I'll have a moment to respond to this." He nodded at the letter, which he proceeded to slip into his pocket, then turned back to the others. He offered his arm to one young woman, other gentlemen attended to other beauties; in a courtly manner the merry company idled up the rose-covered hill.

I slunk along behind them without getting in anyone's way, for nobody paid me any further attention. High spirits reigned among Mr. John's invited guests, they fooled around and told jokes, at times they spoke seriously of lighthearted things, more often making light of serious matters, and took a particular pleasure in poking fun at absent friends and their affairs. I was too much a stranger to grasp all the allusions, too much wrapped up in myself and my own troubles to share in the general merriment.

We had reached the rose bushes. Lovely Fanny, who, it appeared, was everyone's favorite, impetuously reached out and broke off a blossoming sprig of roses, and in the process pricked herself on a thorn; it was as though purple drops fell from the dark rose onto her delicate hand. Everyone was up in arms. English plasters were requested. A quiet, thin, haggard, lanky, aging gentleman who accompanied the others, and whom I had not noticed until then, immediately stuck his hand into the lap pocket of his tight-fitting gray taffeta coat, pulled out a small pouch, opened it, and with a courtly bow, reached in and handed the lady the desired dressing. She accepted it without so much as acknowledging the kindness, let alone thanking the man; she had her wound dressed, and everyone proceeded up the hill, the crest of which afforded a panoramic view that took in the wide green labyrinth of the gardens and swept far out into the immeasurable expanse of the sea.

The view was truly grand and splendid. On the horizon between the darkness of the deep and the powder blue of the sky appeared a light spot. "Somebody hand me a looking glass!" cried Mr. John, and even before the servants could respond to the command, the man in gray bowed humbly, stuck his hand into his coat pocket, pulled out a fine telescope, and handed it to the host. The latter immediately brought it up to his eye and informed his guests that it was the ship that had departed the day before and had been held back by unfavorable winds. The telescope was passed from hand to hand and did not find its way back to its owner. I, however, peered in amazement at the man, wondering how such a large piece of equipment could possibly have emerged from that minuscule pocket. Yet nobody else seemed to take notice; they paid no more attention to the gray man than to myself.

Refreshments were served, the rarest most exotic fruits presented in the most exquisite dishes. Mr. John did the honors without much of a fuss, and for the second time addressed a word to me: “Eat up, my good man, surely you didn’t enjoy such delights at sea.” I bowed in gratitude, but he didn’t notice; he was already involved in conversation with someone else.

The guests expressed the desire to stretch out on the lawn at the crest of the hill with the splendid panoramic view, were it not for the dampness of the ground. How heavenly it would be, someone said, if only we had Turkish rugs to spread out here. No sooner said than done: the man in the gray coat had already slipped a hand into his pocket, and with a modest, indeed downright obsequious, manner, took pains to pull out a gold-embroidered Turkish carpet. Servants took hold of it quite matter-of-factly and spread it out at the desired spot. And without any further ado, the guests sat down. Dumbfounded, I once again stared in amazement at the man, his pocket, the carpet, which measured over twenty feet in length and ten in width. I rubbed my eyes, not knowing what to think of it all, particularly since no one else seemed to find anything out of the ordinary.

I would have liked to have some information about the man, to ask who he was, but I didn’t know whom to ask: for I was almost more intimidated by the servants than I was by those they served. Finally I pulled myself together and approached a young man who seemed of a lesser standing than the others, and who often kept to himself. Quietly I inquired as to the identity of the accomodating gentleman in gray.

"That one over there, the one who resembles a snippet of thread that slipped out of a tailor's needle?"

"Yes, the one standing alone."

"Don't know him," he replied, and to avoid any lengthier exchange with me, he immediately turned away and commenced making small talk with someone else.

The sun was now shining all the more brightly, and this bothered the ladies. Lovely Fanny turned to the gray man, to whom, as far as I could tell, no one had yet addressed a word, and flippantly inquired if he did not perchance also have a tent in his pocket? Responding with a deep bow, as though an undeserved honor had been paid him, he already had his hands in his pocket, and I was witness as he pulled out poles, cords, pikes, in short, everything needed to pitch a magnificent pavilion. The young gentlemen put it up, and it covered the entire length and breadth of the carpet—and not a soul found anything strange in this. I had been flabbergasted from the very beginning, and indeed felt a little queasy; just imagine my state when in response to the next whimsical wish, I saw him pull out three horses—I swear, three big beautiful steeds fitted with saddle and reins! Imagine, for heaven's sake, three saddled steeds pulled from that same pocket out of which a wallet, a telescope, a fine Turkish carpet twenty feet long and ten feet wide, a tent of the same dimensions and all the equipment, poles, and pikes that go with it had already emerged! If I hadn't sworn to it with my own eyes, you surely wouldn't believe me.

As ill at ease and humble as the man appeared, despite the lack of attention he attracted from the others, his pallid presence (to which my eyes were riveted) so revolted me that I could no longer bear to look at him. I decided to slip away unnoticed from this merry company, which, considering the inconsequential role I played in it, promised to be an easy matter. I wanted to make my way back to the city and try my luck again the following morning with Mr. John, and, if I found the courage, to ask him about the strange gray man. If only I had made good my intention!

I had in fact already succeeded in slipping through the rose hedges and down the hill and found myself in an open meadow, when the fear of being spotted sneaking through the grass impelled me to cast a furtive look behind me. Imagine how startled I was to see the man in the gray coat approaching me from behind. He immediately doffed his hat to me and made the deepest bow that anyone had ever made to me. There was no doubt that he wished to speak to me, and I could not possibly avoid him without being outright rude. I too removed my hat, bowed in turn, and stood bareheaded in the blazing sunlight, as if rooted to the ground. I gave him a piercing, terrified look, and felt awfully ill at ease; not looking up at me, he bowed several more times, stepped closer, and addressed me with a quiet, quavering voice and the tone and manner of a beggar.

"The gentleman will please pardon my importunity if I make so bold as to impose my uninvited presence; I have a request. Please be so kind as to forgive me—"

"But for heaven's sake, my good man!" I burst out in terror, "what can I possibly do for a man who—" We both fell silent, and both of us, it seemed to me, turned red at the very same instant.

Following a moment of silence, he once again spoke up. "For the short while during which I enjoyed the pleasure of your proximity, I was struck several times—please permit me to remark upon it—with inexpressible admiration for the lovely, lovely shadow you cast, that shadow you fling to the ground with a certain noble disdain and without the least notice, that lovely shadow lying even now at your feet. Forgive the admitted audacity of such a bold presumption. I wonder if you might possibly consider parting with it—I mean, selling it to me."

He peered at me without uttering another word, and I felt as though a millstone were turning in my head. What was I supposed to make of this odd offer to buy my shadow from me? The man must be mad, I thought, and altering my tone to suit his humble manner, I replied, "Now, now! good friend, isn't your own shadow enough for you? What you propose is a very curious sort of deal."

To which he immediately answered back, "I have here in my pocket certain things that the gentleman may find not altogether lacking in value; the highest sum would be too little to pay for such a priceless shadow."

I felt a chill run down my spine when he reminded me of that pocket, and I deeply regretted having called him my good friend. It was my turn to speak, and I tried with immeasurable tact to retract any hint of intimacy between us. "But my good sir," I said, "you must forgive your most humble servant. I don't quite catch your drift; how could I possibly . . . I mean, my shadow—"

He interrupted me. "I beg the gentleman's consent, if he will permit me here on the spot to pick up and take hold of his noble shadow; how I manage it is my affair. In exchange, as a token of my appreciation, the gentleman may choose from among the treasures I have here in my pocket: the original mandrake wishing root, magic pennies, pirate doubloons, Roland's squire's serviette, a little hangman to be had for a song; but such trinkets are surely not your style: how about Fortunatus's magic hat, restored, good as new; or else a magic purse just like the one he had."

"Fortunatus's magic purse?" I interrupted him, and as much as I shivered with fear in his presence, with those three words he had tapped my wildest dream. I suddenly felt dizzy, my eyes dazzled by the glitter of imagined gold.

"Will the gentleman be so kind as to examine and test the efficacy of this purse." He stuck his hand into his pocket, pulled out a middling large, tightly stitched pouch of strong Spanish leather fastened by two leather straps, and handed it to me.

I reached in and pulled out ten gold pieces out, and another ten, and another; in a flash I extended my hand. "Sold! It's a deal; in exchange for the purse, you can have my shadow."

He shook my hand and without delay crouched down before me, and I watched as with startling skill he peeled and lifted my shadow from head to foot off the grass, rolled it up and folded it, and stuffed it in his pocket. He got up, bowed again, and stepped back toward the rose bushes. It seemed to me as if I heard him quietly laughing to himself. I for my part grasped the purse tightly by its straps; all around me the world was bathed in bright sunlight, and I was oblivious to what I had done.

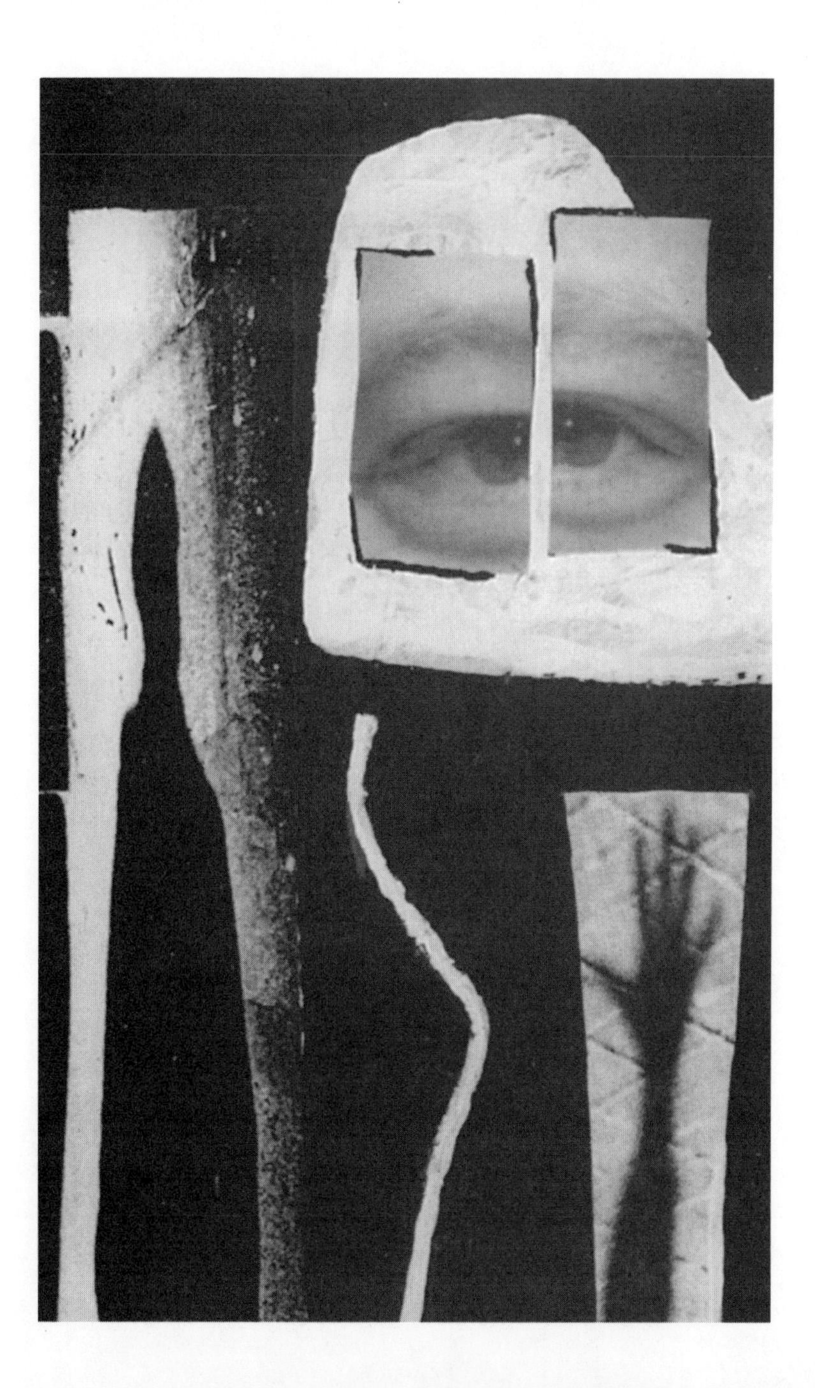

–2–

I finally came to my senses and made haste to leave this place where, I hoped, I had no more business to attend to. First I filled my pockets with gold, then I bound the straps of the purse around my neck and tucked it away under my shirt. Unnoticed, I emerged from the gardens, reached the highway, and headed back to the city. As I approached the gates of the city, lost in thought, I heard a voice calling behind me. "Young man! Heh! Young man! Listen up!" I looked back, and saw an old woman crying out, "Better retrace your steps, sir! The gentleman has lost his shadow!"

"Thanks, Granny!" I replied, and tossed her a gold piece for the well-meant advice, whereupon I sought refuge in the shade of the trees lining the road. At the city gates I was obliged to suffer a repeat performance; the gatekeeper said, "Where did the gentleman leave his shadow?" And right after that, a couple of women remarked aloud, "Heavens, the poor man has no shadow!"

This business was beginning to get on my nerves, so I took pains to avoid sunny places. This, however, was not always possible—not, for instance, when crossing a wide street, which I was obliged to cross, and unfortunately for me, at the very hour when boys were getting out of school. A cursed little hunch-backed rogue—I can still see him now—immediately noticed that I was missing a shadow. This fact he revealed at the top of his lungs to all the children of the neighborhood, who in turn proceeded on the spot to hurl lumps of dirt and deride me: "Honest people don a shadow when they step out into the sun." To get rid of them I tossed handfuls of gold among them and leaped into a carriage, with the assistance of a few sympathetic souls.

I was still quite upset when the carriage pulled up to my old lodgings; the very idea of once again setting foot in my miserable garret was more than I could bear. I had my things brought down, accepted the pathetic bundle with revulsion, scattered a few gold coins, and had the driver take me to the best hotel in town. The establishment faced north, I did not have to fear the effects of sunlight here. I paid the coachman in gold coin, had the hotel prepare its best suite of rooms, and as soon as they were ready I dashed upstairs and locked myself in.

What do you think I did then? Oh my dear friend Chamisso, I am ashamed to admit it even to you of all people. I pulled out that hapless purse from under my shirt and with a fury that flared up in me like a raging fire, I kept plucking out gold and gold and gold and ever more gold, and spread it out over the cold stone floor and trampled through it and let it tinkle underfoot, and kept dropping more and more of it, my poor heart feasting on the glitter and the jingle, piling ever more precious metal on metal, until in a fit of exhaustion I myself sank onto that priceless mattress, and reveling in my riches, I tossed and wallowed in it. This is how I spent the entire day and the evening. I never unlocked my door; by nightfall I was still lying in my gold, and that was where sleep overcame me.

You appeared to me in a dream; it was as if I were standing behind the glass door of your little room and caught a glimpse of you seated there at your desk between a skeleton and a sheaf of dried plants; fat tomes by Haller, Humboldt, and Linnaeus were spread open before you, and on your sofa lay a volume of Goethe and the *Magic Ring*. I looked at you a long while, then at every object in the room, and then at you again; but you remained perfectly still, not drawing a single breath; you were dead.

I awakened. It seemed to be very early still. My watch had stopped. I felt completely exhausted, and thirsty and hungry too at the same time; I hadn't eaten since the previous morning. Sated, and somewhat revolted at the sight of all that gold on which just a little while ago I had gorged my heart, I shoved it aside; now all of a sudden, to my great annoyance, I didn't know what to do with it. I could hardly leave it in full view on the floor; I tried to see if the purse would gobble it back up. Nothing doing. None of my windows opened out onto the sea. I had to make do as best I could; with great effort, sweat dripping from my brow, I managed to lug it over to a huge closet in an adjoining cubicle and temporarily stored it there. I left only a few handfuls lying around.

Once I was done, I dropped exhausted into an easy chair and waited for the sounds of movement in the house. As soon as it seemed possible, I ordered food and asked to see the hotel director. With him I discussed my future affairs—how, for instance, I might go about furnishing a house. He recommended for my personal needs the services of a certain Bendel, whose loyal and compassionate face immediately won me over. He was to be the helpmate whose devotion and sympathetic company have since helped me weather and endure the heavy burden of my dour fate. I spent the entire day in my rooms interviewing prospective servants and dealing with shoemakers, tailors, and merchants. I acquired a wardrobe for myself and bought all manner of valuables and precious stones, just to get rid of a small portion of my store of gold; and yet it seemed as if I could not even make a dent in the heap.

All the while I wavered in a terrible state of the greatest anxiety. I did not dare set foot outside my door, and in the evening I had forty candles lit in my room before I emerged from my dark corner. I remembered with dread that awful encounter with the schoolchildren. Finally I resolved, my fear notwithstanding, once again to test public opinion. It was that time of the month when the moon lights up the night sky. Late in the evening I draped a greatcoat over my shoulders, pulled my hat down low over my eyes, and slipped out into the street, shivering like a common criminal. I sought out a very remote part of town before emerging into the moonlight from the shadow of the houses whose protective darkness had heretofore afforded me refuge; I was prepared to accept the verdict on my fate from the mouths of passing strangers.

Spare me, dear friend, the pain of recounting all that I had to endure. The women in particular often voiced the pity with which my condition suffused their hearts; their remarks cut me to the quick just as much as the jeering of the children and the disdainful scorn of the men, particularly those well-dressed burghers who themselves cast such a broad and imposing shadow. A lovely and gracious girl, who, so it seemed, was out for an evening stroll with her parents, her glance modestly directed downward as was theirs, looked up and cast a bright eye upon me; visibly startled upon noticing my shadowless state, she buried her beautiful face in her veil, let her head sink down, and walked on in silence.

I could not bear it any longer. Salty torrents streamed from my eyes, and reeling with a shattered heart, I withdrew again into darkness. I was obliged to hug the sides of the houses for safety's sake, and proceeding slowly, I finally arrived very late at my lodgings.

I spent a long, sleepless night. The next day, my first concern was to seek out the man in the gray coat. Who knew? I might succeed in finding him again, and how fortunate it would be if, like myself, he too regretted our ill-considered swap. I called for Bendel—he seemed clever and adroit; I described in detail the features of the man who possesssed a treasure without which my life would be nothing but an ordeal. I told him the time and the place where I had seen him last, described all the other people who were present, and added the following detail: he should ask after the telescope, a Turkish carpet interwoven with strands of gold, a magnificent tent, and finally the black stallions, all of which, I implied, were related in some way—though I did not specify just how—to the mysterious stranger of whom no one else at that fateful garden party where I met him appeared to have taken notice, yet who had shattered the peace and joy of my life.

As soon as I had finished speaking, I hauled out as much gold as I could carry, adding diamonds and jewels to the pile to top it off. "Bendel," I said, "money opens many doors and often facilitates the impossible; don't be sparing in your spending, just as I am not, but go and gladden your master's heart with tidings on which his future depends."

He went on his way, returning, dejected, late that evening. None of Mr. John's servants, none of his guests—he had sought out and questioned each and every one—had the faintest recollection of the man in the gray coat. The new telescope was there, but no one could tell where it had come from; the carpet and the tent were still there, spread out on the same hilltop; and the servants lauded the wealth of their master, but none could recall the provenance of these latest acquisitions. Mr. John himself took great pleasure in these new treasures and wasn't troubled by the fact that he had no idea whatsoever where they had come from; the horses were tethered in the stables of the young men who had ridden them on that afternoon, and who were quick to praise Mr. John for his generosity in giving them such fine steeds as gifts. This is what I learned from Bendel's detailed account, and despite the fruitlessness of his efforts, his zeal and adroitness elicited my praise. Sadly, then, I motioned for him to leave me alone with my misery.

"Now that I have informed my master of those matters of greatest importance to him," Bendel continued, "I must still pass on a message. Early this morning, as I was rushing off to attend to the mission that, alas, I have failed to fulfill, a man stopped me at your doorstep and said, 'Be so good as to tell Mr. Peter Schlemiel that he will not see me hereabouts again soon, for I am off to sea, and a fortuitous wind bids me make haste to the harbor. But one year from today I will have the honor of once again looking him up, at which time I hope to offer an attractive business proposition. Please be so kind as to convey my humble respects and assure him of my gratitude.' I asked him his name, but he said you'd know who he was."

"What did he look like?" I inquired apprehensively. And feature for feature, word for word, Bendel proceeded to describe the man in the gray coat, just as he had described him before in his recounting of the unsuccessful search. "Oh unhappy man!" I cried out, wringing my hands, "that was *him!*" and the realization suddenly struck poor Bendel.

"Yes, of course, it was him, in the flesh," he shrieked, "and I, a blind and dimwitted oaf, failed to recognize him, I failed to recognize him, and so have failed my master!"

He burst out weeping, heaping upon himself the bitterest reproaches, and his despair elicited pity from my heart. I comforted him, assured him repeatedly that I had no doubt about his faithfulness, and promptly sent him out to the harbor to hunt down any possible traces of that elusive gentleman. That very morning, however, many ships that had been held back by inauspicious winds set sail, each in a different direction, each bound for a far-flung coast, and the gray man had disappeared without a trace—like a shadow.

–3–

What good would wings do a man shackled in iron chains? He would have to suffer his bondage all the same, and all the more miserably. I lay like Faffner beside his hoard, far removed from the balm of any human consolation, fondling my gold, not lovingly but cursing it all the while—that wretched stuff for the sake of which I had cut myself off from life. Guarding my own dark secret, I feared the lowliest of my servants, whom I also envied; for he had his shadow, he could allow himself to be seen in broad daylight showered by the rays of the sun. Day and night I pined away alone in my rooms, and grief gnawed at my heart.

Meanwhile, another suffering soul ate his heart out before my eyes. My faithful servant Bendel would not stop castigating himself for having betrayed the trust of his good master in failing to recognize the man he had been sent out to find, with whom he believed my unhappy destiny to be bound. I, however, could hardly blame him, for I recognized in this cruel twist of fate the inscrutable nature of the unknown.

Having resolved not to pass up any possible solution to my problem, I sent Bendel with a costly diamond ring to the most renowned portrait painter in town, whom I invited to call on me. Upon his arrival, I dismissed my servants from the room, locked the door, sat myself down beside him, and after praising his work, with a heavy heart I finally came to the point; but first

I made him swear to keep what I was about to tell him a carefully guarded secret.

"Master," I began, "might it be possible to paint a shadow for a man who tragically lost his own?"

"An artificial shadow you mean?"

"Precisely."

"But tell me," he asked, "through what clumsiness, through what negligence might the gentleman have lost his shadow?"

"Just how it happened," I replied, "little; or maybe all too much," and I launched into the following shamefaced lie: "In Russia, where the gentleman went on business last winter, the cold was so bitter that one day his shadow froze to the ground and he was no longer able to pry it loose."

"Any artificial shadow that I might possibly be able to paint for the gentleman he would lose again the moment he makes a move; moreover, let me add that any man so little attached to the shadow he was born with as one must surmise from your sad account had best avoid the sun—that would be the most sensible and fullproof solution." He rose from his chair and bid me farewell, while regarding me with a piercing look that I could not for the life of me endure. I sank back into my chair and buried my face in my hands.

This is how Bendel found me when he entered the room. He witnessed firsthand the pain of his master and wanted quietly, respectfully, to withdraw. I looked up. I felt overcome by the burden of my misery, I simply had to communicate it to someone. "Bendel," I cried out to him, "Bendel! You alone, who see and esteem my sufferings enough not to ask after their source, but appear rather to suffer them with me in silence—come to me, Bendel, and be my bosom friend! I have not hidden from you the storehouse of gold, nor will I hide from you my store of grief. Bendel, don't leave me! Bendel, you see me as a man of wealth, generous, kind-hearted; you imagine that the world ought by rights to honor me, and yet you see me fleeing from the world and locking myself away. Bendel, the world has passed judgment on me and cast me from its midst, and you too may turn away from me once you learn my terrible secret: Bendel, I am rich, generous, good-hearted, but—oh God!—I have no shadow!"

"No shadow?" the good fellow cried out in horror, and tears streamed from his eyes. "Oh, woe is me that I was ever born to serve a shadowless master!" He fell silent, and I held my face in my hands.

"Bendel," I added in a trembling voice, "now that you have my trust you can betray it. Go and denounce me to the world!" He appeared to be locked in a deep struggle with himself; finally he fell down on his knees before me and grasped my hand, which he showered with his tears.

"No," he cried out, "whatever the world may think, I cannot and will not abandon my good master for a mere shadow's sake. I will act justly and not wisely, I will stay with you, I will lend you my own shadow, help you whenever I can, and when I cannot, I will weep with you." I wrapped my arms around his neck, astounded at such an uncommon nobility of spirit, fully convinced that he was not after my gold.

From that day, my fortunes and way of life underwent a change for the better. It would be difficult to describe the lengths to which Bendel went to conceal my infirmity from the world. Wherever I went, he went before me and with me, anticipating any and all eventualities, and where danger threatened unexpectedly, he was quick to cover me with his own shadow, for he was bigger and stronger than I. And so I dared to circulate again among people, and I adopted a role in society. Naturally I was obliged to feign certain peculiarities and moods; but eccentricity is after all the privilege of the rich, and so long as the truth remained hidden, I enjoyed all the honor and respect that money can buy. With a newfound claim to life, I looked forward to the much-anticipated visit of the mysterious stranger a year and a day hence.

I sensed that I had best not stay too long in a place where I had already been spotted without a shadow and could easily be betrayed; it may also well be that the awful memory of my appearance at Mr. John's haunted and troubled me. Thus, I intended to test the waters here, as it were, so as later, in some other place, to appear more self-assured and secure, but vain illusions won out for a while over my better judgement: it's no use casting loose once vanity has dropped anchor.

It was none other than lovely Fanny, the belle of Mr. John's garden party, whom I met again at the third town in which I stopped, and who, without remembering ever having seen me before, now paid me some attention—for suddenly I was charming and witty. When I opened my mouth, people listened, and I myself had no idea how I had acquired the art of directing and dominating a conversation. The impression I seemed to have made on that stunning creature turned me into precisely what she wanted me to be, an infatuated fool, and I pursued her thereafter with a thousand little attentions, seeking the refuge of shadows and sunset wherever possible. I was vain enough to want to make her vain about me, and could not with the best of intentions drive the rapture from my head to my heart.

But why repeat the entire sordid tale for you? You yourself have recounted it often enough of other honored personnages. To the age-old comedy, in which I willingly accepted a hackneyed role, I added a homespun hint of tragedy, thereby hastening the catastrophe that was so unexpectedly to befall me.

One lovely evening, as was my wont, having assembled a merry gathering in my garden, I wandered off some distance from the others arm in arm with the fair Fanny, and took great pains to churn out witticisms. In a ladylike fashion, she gazed at the ground and quietly replied in kind to each squeeze of her tiny hand; then without warning, the moon emerged from behind a cloud — and she saw that only ***her*** shadow was cast on the lawn. Aghast, she looked up at me in horror, then down at the ground again, searching for my absent shadow; and her train of thought was so legible in her troubled look that I would have burst out in loud laughter had a cold chill not then and there run down my spine.

I let her fall from my arms in a faint, sped like an arrow through the party of horrified guests, reached the gate, threw myself into the first carriage I could flag down, and drove back to the city, where this once (to my great misfortune) I had left the vigilant Bendel behind. He looked aghast when he saw me; one word from me said it all. We ordered a team of horses on the spot. I took only one of my servants with me, a clever conniver named Rascal who succeeded through his guile in making himself indispensible to me, and who could not possibly have had any knowledge of the incident that prompted my departure. I put thirty miles behind me that very night. Bendel stayed behind to liquidate my holdings, distribute the necessary funds, and pack up the essentials. When he caught up with me the following day, I threw myself into his arms and swore to him never to commit such a folly again, but to be more careful in the future. We hastened on our way without stopping till we got to the border and crossed a mountain, and only on the far side of the ridge, with nature's bulwark between me and that unlucky place, did I permit myself to rest from the burdensome memory; and so we stopped at a nearby and little-frequented spa.

–4–

To make a long story short, I will, alas, be obliged to pass quickly over a period in the reminiscence of which I would—only too gladly—like to linger, could I but thereby conjure up the ghost of living memory. But the true colors that once gave life to that glorious interlude, colors whose hue alone can resurrect it—those tints have been washed away by time. To seek them out again in the faded palette of my emotions, to dredge up the pain and joy and gentle madness that once made my chest heave—that would be like foolishly striking a boulder in search of a stream that has long since dried up, a parched wellspring abandoned by God. How changed is the bygone time that peers back at me now! It is like a play in which I ought to have tackled an heroic role, yet being ill-prepared, a neophyte on stage, I let myself be distracted from my performance, smitten hopelessly by a pair of blue eyes in the crowd. Her parents, taken in by my charade, pull out all the stops, offer me everything just to make the match, and clinch the deal as quickly as possible. And this common farce ends in scorn for the unwitting clown. And that is all, all there is to tell! My words sound fatuous and insipid, and how terrible that the very past that once stirred such profound feeling in my breast could be reduced to this—O Mina! Just as I wept when I lost you back then, I weep now, having lost the shimmer of your memory in me. Has age caught up with me? Oh, wretched reason! Grant me but one more flutter of that fleeting bliss, a moment of sweet madness—but no! I float alone on the bitter, barren foam of time and tide, and have long since downed the last drop of champagne from my goblet!

I had sent Bendel on ahead with several sacks of gold to rent and furnish lodgings for me according to my needs. The good man had scattered much money about, and spoken in the vaguest terms of the noble stranger he served, for I did not wish to be known by name. This heavy veil of mystery gave the good townspeople some curious ideas. As soon as my house was ready for me to move in, Bendel came to fetch me, to accompany me personally to my new home. The two of us set out together.

About an hour's ride from our destination, on a wide sunny plain, the road was blocked by a crowd decked out in festive finery. The carriage halted. Music, church bells, cannon fire could be heard in the distance, and a loud hurrah rang out in the crowd. A chorus of young girls of exceptional beauty, all dressed in white, advanced toward us, one of whom outshone the others, who faded in her wake like the stars of the night sky in the wake of the rising sun. She stepped forth from among her sisters, and this lofty delicate apparition knelt down before me, her face flushed crimson. She held out to me on a silken cushion a wreath of braided laurel, olive branch, and roses, and proceeded to declaim a few choice words about majesty, reverence, and love, words I did not understand, but whose enchanting silvery timbre bewitched my ear and my heart—and it seemed to me as if this heavenly apparition had once before wafted past me. The virginal chorus broke out in an ode to a good king and the happiness of his subjects.

And all this big to-do, dear friend, in broad daylight! There she was, kneeling two steps in front of me, and I, for lack of a shadow, could not bridge the gap between us, could not fall to my knees before that angel. Oh, what wouldn't I have given at that moment for a shadow! I had to keep my shame, my fear, and my desperation buried deep in the darkness of my carriage. Bendel finally took the initiative, acting on my behalf; he leaped out of his side of the carriage, but I called him back in the nick of time, and reaching into my jewel box, fished out the first object my fingers happened to touch, a diamond tiara that I had intended to give the lovely Fanny, and handed it to him. He stepped forward, and spoke in the name of his master, who neither sought nor desired such reverential treatment—said Bendel; there must be some mistake, but let the good townspeople nevertheless be thanked for their kindness. Thereupon he took up the proffered wreath from its silken pillow and laid the diamond tiara in its place; then he graciously extended a hand to the young girl to rise, and with another courtly sweep of the hand dispensed with the local curate, magistrate and other prominent officials. No one else was permitted to approach me.

Bendel motioned for the throng to part and make room for the horses, swung himself back up into the carriage, and off we went at a gallop, passing under a canopy of wreaths and flowers into the city, while the cannons kept firing in our honor. The carriage stopped in front of my new house; I leapt nimbly past the crowd of onlookers whose curiosity had brought them to my doorstep, and bounded through the door. The crowd hailed me with hurrahs outside my windows and I let gold ducats rain down on them. That evening, of course, the whole town was lit up in celebration.

And I still had no idea what all the to-do was about and who they thought I was. I sent Rascal out to make inquiry. He heard, as he later informed me, that the King of Prussia was traveling through those parts under the assumed alias of a count; that my servant Bendel had supposedly been recognized, revealing his and my identities; and finally, that the townspeople were jubilant to have me settle in their midst. Fathoming at last that I had clearly wished to maintain a strict incognito, they regretted having so impetuously penetrated my disguise. Yet His Highness had responded with such mercy and grace, surely he would forgive the good hearts of his subjects.

My rogue of a servant found the whole thing so amusing that he did his best, by words of warning dropped for effect, to confirm the people's suspicion. He delivered a hilarious report, and since his delivery made me laugh, he took full advantage of the situation to win me over with his practiced guile. Must I admit it? It flattered me to have my lowly person mistaken for the lofty countenance of the king.

For the following evening, I ordered a great feast to be prepared in the shade of the trees in front of my house, to which I invited the entire city. Thanks to the mysterious potential of my purse, Bendel's efforts, and Rascal's quick-witted inventiveness, we succeeded in beating the clock. It is astounding what lavish splendor and beauty we were able to fabricate in a few hours. The extravagance and the excess conjured up! Even the ingenious lighting was so shrewdly distributed that I could move about with ease. My servants had thought of everything, and I had only to distribute well-earned praise.

Evening set in. The guests appeared, and were presented to me. The matter of my purported majesty was never mentioned again, but I was addressed with deep reverance and humility as Sir Count. What was I to do? I let the title stick, and became from that moment Count Peter. Yet amid all that festive fanfare, my soul yearned for her. She came late, she who was and who wore the crown. She followed her parents demurely, and did not seem to know that she was the reigning beauty. The forest warden and his wife and daughter were presented to me. I managed to say many fine and fitting things to the old gentleman, yet before his daughter I stood in awe like a tongue-tied schoolboy and couldn't bring a single word to my lips. Finally, stammering, I bid her honor this occasion and asked her to carry out the duties commensurate with the crown she wore. With a stirring look and blushing with shame, she asked me to excuse her; but still more ashamed before her than she was before me, I offered my respects as her most humble servant, and a wink from the Count served as a command to all present to commence the revelries, a command that my obedient subjects were quick and eager to carry out. Majesty, Innocence, and Grace aligned with Beauty decreed a joyous celebration. Mina's jubilant parents felt honored by the honor done their child; I myself was in indescribable ecstasy. I ordered all the jewels I had left, all the pearls, all the diamonds, all the precious stones I had purchased just to get rid of some of my gold to be set out in two covered bowls and passed around in the name of the queen of the day to all her ladies-in-waiting; and meanwhile, handfuls of gold were tossed throughout the evening, over the barriers that had been erected, into the cheering masses.

Next morning Bendel took me aside and revealed to me in confidence his long-held doubt concerning Rascal's reliability, a doubt recently confirmed by the certainty of his guilt. Just yesterday he had discovered whole sacks of gold in Rascal's possession. "Let us not begrudge the poor rogue his little stash of booty," I replied; "my generosity extends to everyone else, why not to him too? Yesterday he served me well, as did all the new servants you found for me; they joyously helped me celebrate a joyous occasion."

We spoke no more of this matter. Rascal remained my majordomo, but Bendel was my friend and confidant. Bendel had grown accustomed to regarding my wealth as limitless, and he did not seek out its source; rather, he helped me, in accordance with my own inclinations, to think up a multitude of delightful ways to spend it. But of that mysterious figure, the man in gray, that pale-faced weasel who was the bane of my existence, he knew only this much: Through him alone could I be released from the curse that weighed so heavily upon me; in him alone, whom I most feared, did my one hope lie. I should add that I was quite convinced that he for his part could find me anywhere but that I could find him nowhere, and therefore, patiently awaiting the promised day, I forswore any further attempts to track him down.

My comportment and the lavish splendor of the party I had given at first confirmed the unsuspecting local citizenry in their foregone conviction as to my true identity. Soon thereafter, newspapers reported that the entire business concerning the fabulous journey of the King of Prussia through those parts was mere unsubstantiated rumor. Yet, once anointed monarch in the popular imagination, a monarch I was bound to remain, and moreover, one of the richest and most regal monarchs the world had ever known—though no one could say for certain over what realm I ruled. Still, the world has never had grounds to complain of a lack of kings, least of all in these times; the good people, who had never actually seen a king with their own eyes, traced my provenance now to this place, now to that—Count Peter, in any case, remained Count Peter. Once there appeared among the transient guests of our little spa town a merchant who had declared himself bankrupt only to recoup his fortune, a man who enjoyed public esteem and cast a broad, albeit somewhat pallid, shadow. He wished to make a public display of the wealth he had amassed, and he even had the ill-advised notion of challenging me to measure my fortune against his. I had only to reach into my trusty purse; soon I had the poor braggart so badly beaten that he had once again to declare bankruptcy just to save face, after which he fled in disgrace across the mountains. So I was rid of him. I admit that I attracted the attention of many ne'er-do-wells and idlers in the region.

With all the splendor and extravagance of my festivities, I maintained a very simple household regime and lived apart from the world. I made the most fastidious caution my rule; under no circumstances was anyone but Bendel allowed to enter my private rooms. As long as the sun shone in the sky, I remained locked away with Bendel as my sole companion; word had it that the count was busy at his desk. In accordance with these arrangements, I had a steady stream of couriers charged with any trifle continuously coming and going. I received guests only in the evening under my trees or in my great hall, which was brightly illuminated according to Bendel's instructions. And when I went out, with Bendel watching over me like a hawk, my destination was always the forest warden's garden, to see *her;* for love alone plucked at my heartstrings and gave me the will to live.

O my dear old friend Chamisso, I hope that you have not forgotten what love is! I will let you fill in the details here as you see fit. Mina was truly a lovable, kind, and devoted child. I had

drawn her heart and her soul to mine; modest as she was, she had no idea how she had earned the honor of my attentions, and with all the youthful energy of an innocent heart, she returned love for love. She loved in every way just like a woman, giving her all: forgetting herself, dedicating herself without reservation to the man who was her life, even if it meant her own demise; in short, it was true love.

But I, on the other hand—oh, what awful hours I spent!—awful! and yet well worth wishing back—how often I wept on Bendel's breast after the first unconscious raptures of love had subsided, when I came to my senses and cast a sharp eye upon myself. How could I, a man without a shadow, so selfishly and deceitfully corrupt such an angel, besmirch and filch her pure soul! At first I resolved to reveal to her the truth about myself; then I swore with solemn oaths to tear myself away from her and escape; then I broke down in tears all over again, forgot my resolve, and made arrangements with Bendel that very evening to visit the forest warden's garden.

At times I deceived myself, putting great store in the imminent visit of the gray stranger, and then I wept again and gave up all hope. I had calculated the day on which I was once again to meet that awful man; for he had said it would be a year and a day, and I took him at his word.

Mina's parents were kind, honorable old folk who loved their only child very much; the nature of our involvement, once they fathomed the depth of emotion Mina and I already felt for each other, came as a total surprise to them, and they didn't know what to do. They would never have dreamed that Count Peter might so much as blink an eye at their child; now he was in love with her, and was loved by her in return. The mother was indeed vain enough to imagine the possibility of a match and to work toward that end, but the old man's healthy common sense could not countenance such far-fetched aspirations. Both were in any case convinced of my pure intentions; they could do nothing but pray for their child. I still have a letter that Mina wrote me back then. Here it is! Word for word!

"What a weak and foolish girl I am—just to imagine that because I love him so very very much, my beloved would not want to hurt me.—Dear heart, you are so good, so unspeakably good to me; but you mustn't, mustn't sacrifice anything for me; O God! how I could hate myself if you ever were to do such a thing. No—you have already made me so immeasurably happy. You taught me how to love you. But enough of this nonsense.—I know what lies in store for me, Count Peter belongs not to me but to the world. I'll be proud just to hear: That was him, and that was him again, and this is what he achieved; and that those people revere him and others worship him. You see, just let me start thinking these thoughts, and I could be furious with you for forgetting your proud destiny in the arms of a simple-minded child.

"Enough! Better stop, or the thought of you may yet make me sad, you, oh you! who have made me so happy, so very happy. Have I not also woven an olive branch and a rosebud in your life, as in the wreath that I was privileged to pass to you? I will always have you here in my heart, my beloved, so don't be afraid to leave me. Dear God, I could die, you've made me happy, so unspeakably happy."

You can well imagine how these words cut me to the quick. I tried to explain to her that I was not who people thought I was, that I was nothing but a rich, if miserable, man. A curse was upon me the nature of which would have to remain a secret between us for the moment, since I had not yet given up all hope of its being lifted. This curse was the poison of my days; and heaven forbid that I drag her along with me into the abyss, she who was the only light, the only joy, the very heartbeat of my life. Then she wept again at my unhappiness. Dear God, she was so loving, so good! Just to save me a single tear, that blessed child, she would have sacrificed herself. In truth, she was far from fathoming the real meaning of my words; she imagined me to be the scion of a noble dynasty, a grand and respected ruler struck down by some ill-fated happenstance, and her active imagination sketched out an elaborate heroic backdrop for the portrait of her beloved.

Once again I said to her, "Mina, dear, the last day of the coming month may alter and decide my fate; if things go badly, then I must die, for I could not bear to make you unhappy." She buried her tear-stained face in my arms. "Should destiny rule in your favor, just let me know that you are well, I have no claim on you. But if misery is to be your lot, then bind me to you so that I may help you bear it."

"My dear girl, take back those rash and foolish words—do you know the misery of which you speak, can you picture the curse? Do you know who your beloved—who he—is? Can't you see how I'm standing here shuddering before you, carrying the burden of a terrible secret?" She fell sobbing at my feet, and with solemn oaths repeated her plea.

To the forest warden, who at that very moment happened upon us, I declared my intention of asking for his daughter's hand in marriage on the first day of the next month. I specified the time and date, explaining that certain things might happen between now and then that could have a hand in my fate. The only certainty was my love for his daughter.

The good man was considerably taken aback to hear such words from the mouth of Count Peter. He hugged me to him, and immediately thereafter felt mightily ashamed to have lost control of himself. Then doubt entered his mind, followed by deliberation and paternal concern; he spoke of the dowry, of security, and of his worry above all for the future of his beloved child. I thanked him for bringing all these matters to my attention. I informed him that I wished to settle permanently here where I appeared to be so popular, and that I hoped to lead a carefree life. I bid him acquire in his daughter's name the finest properties available in the area, and to charge the purchase price to me. It was in this way, I said, that a father could best serve the happy couple. This gave him much to do, as wherever he turned, some stranger had good land to offer; he restricted himself to the purchase of a mere million worth of property.

I occupied him with this as an innocent ploy to get him out of our way for a while; I had already used other such ploys, for I must admit that the old man could become a little tiresome. The mother, on the other hand, was somewhat deaf, and not, like her husband, avidly eager to entertain the count.

The mother then came out to join us, and together the old people urged me to stay a while longer, but I did not have a moment to lose, for already I spotted the moon rising over the horizon. My time was up.

The following evening, I once again set out for the forest warden's garden. I had draped my coat broadly over my shoulders and pulled my hat down low over my eyes as I eagerly approached Mina. When she looked up and saw me, she started back with an involuntary jerk: then it came to me again, the specter of that terrible night on which I had shown myself in the moonlight without a shadow. It was she, no doubt about it. But did she put two and two together and realize who I was? She grew silent and reflective. My worry weighed like a millstone on my chest; I sat down, and got up again. Silently weeping, she threw herself into my arms. I took my leave.

After that, I often found her in tears; I myself sank ever deeper into the darkness of my soul. Only her parents seemed to swim in boundless jubilation; the fateful day drew near, dark and dreadful as a storm cloud. Then it was the night before. I could scarcely draw a breath. I had prudently filled several chests with gold, just in case; I lay awake awaiting midnight. At last the clock struck twelve.

Eyes glued to the hands of the clock, each passing minute like a dagger thrust in my heart, I sat there, starting at the slightest sound. And so I welcomed daybreak. The leaden hours rolled on, one, two, three, each displaced by the next; then it was noon, evening, night; the clock hands shifted, hope faded; the clock struck eleven, and no one appeared; the last minutes of the last hour of the day ticked by, and still no one; the first stroke of midnight, the twelfth stroke, and I fell back soaking the cover of my couch in desperate and unending tears. For tomorrow I, an ill-fated shadowless man, was to ask for the hand of my beloved. Toward morning a heavy sleep finally pressed my eyes shut.

–5–

It was still early when I awoke to the sound of heated voices raised in a quarrel in my antechamber. I listened carefully. Bendel stood at my door blocking entry, as Rascal, swearing up and down that he would take no orders from a mere lackey, demanded entry into my room. Kind-hearted Bendel warned him that should such words reach my ears, he would risk the loss of a very favorable position. Rascal threatened to use force if Bendel continued to bar his entry.

I threw on some clothes, angrily flung open the door and spoke to Rascal in a rage. "What do you want with me, you lout?"

He stepped back two paces and responded coldly, "What I want, sir, is to humbly request that you show me your shadow—the sun is just up, and shining so brightly in the yard."

I stood there shaken to the core. It took me awhile to find words. "How in heaven's name can a servant speak so . . . so . . . so rudely to his master—?"

He calmly and quietly replied, "A servant can stand on his honor and refuse to serve a shadowless master. I demand forthwith my release, and tender my resignation."

I was forced to try another tack. "But Rascal, dear Rascal, who ever gave you such a ridiculous idea? How can you even think— ?"

He continued in the same tone of voice: "Certain people claim that you have no shadow, sir—in short, either show me your shadow or hand me my release."

Pale and trembling, but with more presence of mind than I had at the moment, Bendel motioned to me. I sought to appease Rascal with the gold I had lying about; that too had lost its power. He threw it back at my feet: "I take no alms from a shadowless man." He spun round on his heels, put his hat on his head, and slowly waltzed out the door, whistling a tune. Motionless and without a thought in my mind as if turned to stone, I stood staring after him with Bendel at my side.

With a heavy sigh and death in my heart, I finally pulled myself together, and slinking along like a thief preparing to face judgment, I made my way to the forest warden's garden. I stepped through the shady bower that had been named after me, and where no doubt I was expected. The old mother came toward me carefree and cheerful as ever. Mina sat there, pale and lovely as the first snow that sometimes in late autumn bestows a kiss on the last flowers of summer before melting into bitter dew. The forest warden paced up and down, clutching a handwritten note, and appeared to be doing his best to repress a surge of emotion that erupted the moment he spotted me, now in a flush of red, now in a deathlike pallor clouding his otherwise lackluster face. He approached me as I entered the garden and haltingly requested a word with me alone. The allée along which he invited me to follow him led to an open, sunny corner of the garden. Without a word I sank on a bench. A long silence followed that not even the kindly mother dared break.

The forest warden kept pacing with uneven steps up and down the bower; suddenly he came up to me and stood before me in a numb silence, staring down at the sheet of paper in his hand. With a piercing look, he asked me, "I wonder, Sir Count, if you may not be acquainted with a certain Peter Schlemiel?" I said nothing. "A man of impeccable character and incomparable gifts." He clearly expected an answer.

"And what if I myself happened to be he?"

"The man," he added with a dark intensity, "who misplaced his shadow!"

"I knew it, I knew it!" cried Mina, "I've known it for a long time, he has no shadow!" And with that she threw herself into the arms of her horrified mother, who held her close, reproaching her for having kept such an unhappy secret to herself. But like Arethusa, the poor girl became a fountain of tears that erupted at the sound of my voice, gushing forth uncontrollably at my approach and accompanied by convulsive sobs.

"How could you," the forest warden went on angrily, "how could you have the utter gall to deceive this dear girl and me in such an unscrupulous manner; you who claim to love her, and have dragged her so low? See how she's weeping and wringing her hands! What an awful thing you've done!"

I was in such a state that I started talking nonsense. "A shadow is after all nothing but a shadow," I said, "one can just as well do without it, why make such a fuss?" And yet I felt so profoundly the insincerity of my words that I cut myself short without waiting for an answer. I did, however, point out that a thing lost may yet be found again.

The old man replied in anger, "Admit it, sir, 'fess up to the truth! How did you lose your shadow?"

I had to invent another lie. "Why, not so very long ago, an uncouth burly fellow stamped so vehemently on my shadow that he tore a big hole in it. I was obliged to have it repaired—money talks, you know; I was supposed to get it back from the tailor yesterday."

"Well and good, well and good!" the forest warden replied. "You've come a-courting my daughter; well, you're not the only one. As her father, I must look out for her best interests. I give you three days to acquire a shadow; if in three days' time you appear here before me wearing a well-fitting shadow, you will be welcome; but on the fourth day—mark my word!—my daughter will be wed to another." I still wanted to say something to Mina, but she clasped her mother's hand all the more tightly and sobbed all the louder, so that the old woman silently motioned to me to make myself scarce. I staggered off, and it was as if the world itself were closing its gates behind me.

Having eluded Bendel's loving vigilance, I ran through the forests and fields at a mad clip. The cold sweat of terror ran down my brow, I heaved an abysmal sigh, my mind tottered on the brink of madness.

I can't say how much time elapsed before I found myself in a sunny field. I felt a tug at my sleeve. Standing stock-still, I looked around. It was the man in the gray coat, who appeared to be out of breath from chasing after me. He immediately spoke up.

"I announced my arrival for this very day, but you were too impatient to wait. Don't worry, my friend, it's not too late. Take my advice—for a fair trade you can have your shadow back and do an immediate about-face in your life. The forest warden will welcome you back with open arms, and this whole unhappy business will be treated as a bad joke. And that Rascal who betrayed you and who this very minute is wooing your bride-to-be, I'll take him into my service where he belongs—the fellow's ripe for the picking."

In a daze, I repeated his words. "Announced your arrival for this very day—?" I mentally recalculated the allotted time. He was right, I had been a day off. With my right hand, I felt for the purse dangling under my shirt against my breast. He immediately guessed my intent and stepped back two paces.

"Oh no, Sir Count, the purse is in good hands as it is, it's yours to keep." Astonished, I gave him a befuddled, questioning look, to which he replied forthwith, "All I ask for is a little token, a memento, if you will: Your signature, sir, on this document will do." And on the parchment he held in his hands I read the following:

"By my signature I empower the recipient of this parchment to take full claim to my soul following its natural separation from my body."

Dumbfounded, I kept looking back and forth between the document and the gray stranger. Meanwhile, with a freshly cut quill, he proceeded to dab the open wound a thorn had torn in my hand, wet the tip with a drop of my blood, and passed the pen to me.

"Who in God's name are you?" I asked at last.

"What difference does it make?" he replied. "Can't you tell by looking at me? I'm just a poor devil, a sort of sage and alchemist who gets little thanks from his friends for his incomparable wizardry exercised on their behalf, and whose sole pleasure on earth is a little experimentation. But hurry up and sign before the blood dries up. Bottom right: Peter Schlemiel."

I shook my head and said, "Forgive me, sir, this document I cannot sign."

"Not sign?" he repeated, surprised. "But why not?"

"It seems a somewhat questionable transaction, to exchange my soul for my shadow."

"Questionable indeed!" he replied, and broke into loud, sarcastic laughter. "And if I may ask, what sort of thing is that, your soul? Have you ever seen it? What possible use do you intend to make of it once you're dead? You ought to be pleased to have found a collector during your lifetime who's willing to buy the nebulous bequest of X, that galvanic force of polarizing potential, or whatever you prefer to call that ridiculous thing; a collector who proposes to take that tenuous trifle off your hands in exchange for something real, namely, your shadow, the very thing you need to attain the hand of your beloved and make all your dreams come true. Or would you rather be the one to hand her over—nay! to veritably *push* that poor young thing into the arms of that lowdown scoundrel, Rascal? No, my friend, better see it for yourself; here then, let me lend you this magic hood" (he pulled something out of his pocket) "and together we'll make our way unseen to the forest warden's garden."

I must admit that I felt terribly ashamed to be derided by this man. I loathed him from the depth of my heart, and it was this personal revulsion, I believe, much more than any principles or prejudices, that prevented me from buying back my shadow, however much I needed it, for the price of that signature. How distasteful, the very thought of accepting his proposition to take a stroll together! Just the idea of seeing that slimy weasel, that snickering devil, standing between me and my beloved, two bleeding hearts torn asunder—that was more than I could bear. What's done is done, I decided, and turning to the man, I said, "Sir, I did indeed sell you my shadow for this admittedly splendid purse, and I have come ruefully to regret it. In God's name, will you take it back!" He shook his head and gave me a very dark look. So I continued, "In that case, I have no intention of selling you any more of what's mine, be it for the price of my shadow, and I cannot, I'm afraid, sign the contract. And fur-

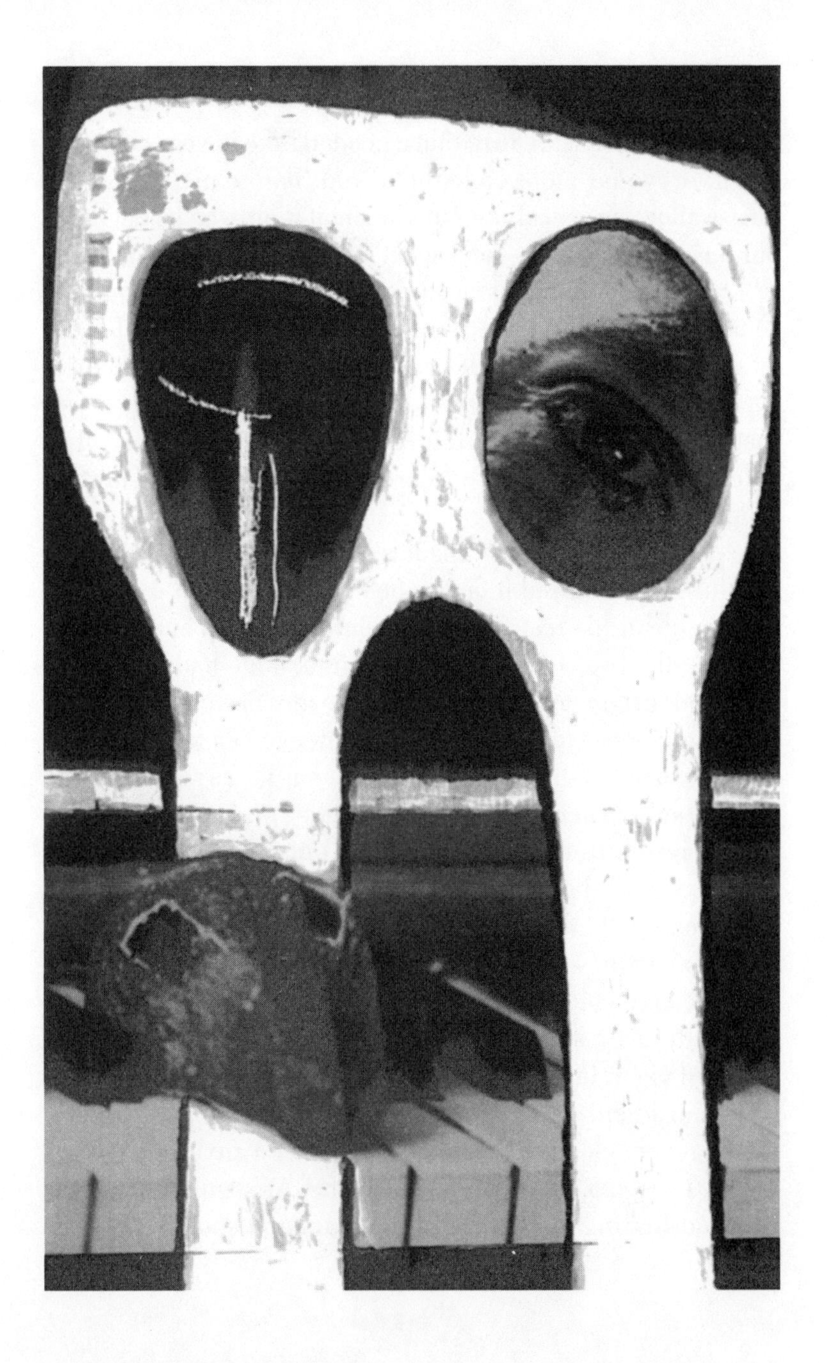

thermore, you must realize that a hooded hike in your company would prove far more amusing to you than to me; therefore, please allow me to decline your kind invitation, which concludes our business together—and so let us go our separate ways!"

"I regret very much, Monsieur Schlemiel, that you should be so thick-headed as to reject out of hand the proposition I made as a token of friendship. Better luck next time, then. I do hope we will meet again soon! Oh, by the way, permit me to show you that I by no means let the things I buy grow musty, but rather take great pains to preserve them—please be assured of my fastidious care!"

He proceeded to pull my shadow out of his pocket, and with a skillful toss, unfurled it on the heath and spread it out on the sunny side at his feet so that he could stride up and down in between the two shadows, his and mine; mine had to obey, to twist and turn in accordance with his every move. When I first caught a glimpse of my poor shadow after such a long time and saw it reduced to such a lowly purpose—as for its sake I too was made to suffer such unspeakable misery—my heart broke, and I burst into bitter tears. That hateful man proudly paraded around with his booty and shamelessly repeated his offer:

"You can still have it for the asking; just a stroke of the pen and His Highness the Count can save his poor unhappy Mina from the claws of that lout, Rascal, and take her in his arms—as I said, just a stroke of the pen." My tears burst forth with renewed vigor, but I turned away and with a wave of my hand bade him adieu.

At that very moment Bendel, who had been anxiously following my footsteps, appeared on the scene. As soon as that faithful, God-fearing man found me in tears and spotted my shadow—for it was unmistakably mine—in the thrall of that awful gray stranger, he immediately resolved to get back for me what was mine, even if by force, and since he had no idea of how to grasp the insubstantial thing itself, he let fly a flurry of angry words and without beating about the bush, demanded that the shadow be returned to its rightful owner. In lieu of an answer, the stranger simply turned his back on my innocent defender, whereupon Bendel raised the thorny club in his hand and followed hot on the gray man's heels, repeating his demand to give up the shadow, pummeling him mercilessly with all his might. The latter, as though well accustomed to such treatment, merely ducked his head, hunched his shoulders, and calmly, quietly continued on his way across the heath, robbing me of both my shadow and my faithful servant. For the longest time, I heard the dull thud resounding until finally it faded in the distance. I was all alone again with my bitter fate.

–6–

Alone on the barren moor, I let loose a torrent of tears, relieving my heart if but for a moment of the inexpressible burden of my fate. I saw no end to the misery that overwhelmed me, no exit, no way out, and I sucked with a grim thirst on the new poison that stranger had poured into my wounds. When I pictured Mina in my mind's eye and her dear sweet face appeared to me pale and drowned in tears, as I had last seen her in the hour of my disgrace, Rascal's impudent, sneering visage stepped between us; I buried my face in my hands and ran wildly across the desolate terrain, but I couldn't shake loose that terrible spectre, it followed me wherever I fled, until, breathless, I sank to the ground and once again burst into tears.

And all for the sake of a shadow! And the mere stroke of a pen could buy me that shadow back! I mulled over the stranger's disconcerting proposition, as well as my reluctance. My mind was a blur, I had lost all capacity to judge or comprehend.

The day drew to an end. I stilled my hunger with wild berries, my thirst in a mountain stream; night fell, and I took refuge under a tree. The damp dawn woke me from a heavy sleep, in which I had overheard my own death rattle. Bendel must have lost my trail, and I was glad of it; I wanted nothing more to do with my fellow man, from whom I had fled in terror like the frightened beasts of the wild. Three desolate days I spent in hiding.

On the morning of the fourth day I found myself on a sandy plain on which the sun shone brightly. I was seated on a pile of rocks with the sun in my face, for I now craved the very sunbath I had so long done without. My heart supped in silence on the source of my despair. Then a faint sound startled me; prepared for escape, I cast a furtive look around. I saw no one: and yet, on the sunny stretch of sand, a human shadow came ambling by, a shadow not unlike my own, a shadow strolling all alone, which appeared to have lost its master.

Then a mighty urge arose in me. Shadow, thought I, if it's a master you're searching for, consider me him. And I leaped forward in an attempt to overtake it. I was convinced, you see, that if I succeeded in stepping into its path so that it made contact with my feet, the shadow would remain stuck there and in time grow accustomed to me.

But as I advanced, the shadow took flight, and I was obliged to give wearisome chase to that fleet-footed quarry. Only the thought of my intolerable condition gave me the energy to press on. The elusive fugitive was heading for a forest in the distance, in the shade of which I would naturally have lost him. The prospect of his escape made my heart flutter with horror, sharpened my resolve, accelerated my pace. I was visibly gaining on him, coming closer and closer—I simply had to catch him. Then suddenly he stopped and turned to me. Like the lion upon its prey, I bounded with a mighty leap to make him mine—and struck unexpectedly against physical resistance. From no visible source I received the most violent jabs in the ribs that ever a man endured.

Fear impelled me involuntarily to clamp shut my arms before me, seizing the unseen presence. That swift gesture made me lunge forward and tumble to the ground; only now did the man lying beneath me prone on his back, and whom I held fast, become visible. Now the whole mysterious business became eminently clear to me. That man must first have been carrying, then dropped, the magic invisible bird's nest, the one that renders invisible whoever happens to be holding it, but not his shadow. I cast a long look around and soon discovered the shadow of the invisible bird's nest, bounded up and at it, and captured my precious prey. Invisible and shadowless, I held the nest in my hands.

The unfortunate man, now starkly visible on the wide sunny plain, sat up forthwith and peered about, looking for the thief, but spotted neither him nor his shadow; the absence of the latter made him particularly anxious. Fleeing from me, he failed to notice, and could hardly be expected to imagine that I was shadowless to begin with. Once he had convinced himself that there was neither hide nor hair of me in sight, he took out his extreme consternation on himself, and tugged and tore at his hair in despair. I, on the other hand, was invigorated by this newly acquired treasure, which gave me at once the ability and the desire once again to seek out human company. I was perfectly inured to any sense of guilt, and felt neither the slightest remorse at having committed an act of common thievery nor the need to excuse myself, and so as to elude any guilt-engendering train of thought, I hurried off without looking back at the poor unfortunate, whose piteous cries kept echoing in my ears. This, at any rate, is how it all seemed to me at the time.

I was burning with desire to return to the forest warden's garden to find out for myself the truth of what the hateful one had revealed to me, but I had no idea where I was. I clambered up a nearby hill to take a look around. From the top of hill I spotted the little town a mere stone's throw away, and the forest warden's garden lying right there at my feet. My heart started pounding furiously, and tears of another sort from those I had lately shed welled up: I was going to see her again. A longing full of misgivings quickened my step as I went bounding down the pathway to her house. I passed unnoticed a group of peasants on their way home from town. They spoke of me, of Rascal, and of the forest warden; I did not want to hear what they had to say, and hurried on.

I entered the garden with the horror of anticipation seething in my breast. The sound of laughter rang out in my ear; shuddering, I cast a quick look around. There was no one in sight. I stepped forward and heard what seemed like the sound of footsteps nearby, but no one was there: My ears must be deceiving me, I thought. It was still early, no one was up and about in Count Peter's arbor, the garden was still deserted; I hastened down the familiar paths and made my way to the house. The same sound, now more distinct, kept following me. With a trembling heart I sat down on an empty bench in a sunny niche facing the front door. I swear I heard that unseen devil laughing scornfully as he sat himself down beside me. A key turned in the lock, the door opened, the forest warden stepped out with papers in hand. I felt as though a fog had descended over my head, I looked around, and—horror of horrors!—the man in the gray coat was seated there beside me eying me with a satanic grin. He had draped his magic hood over his head and mine, and at his feet his shadow and mine lay peacefully side by side. He fiddled absently with the sheet of parchment in his hand, and as the forest warden started pacing up and down in the shadow of the arbor with his own papers in hand, he leaned forward with an air of familiarity and whispered in my ear:

"You really ought to have accepted my invitation, we'd only be seated as we are now, two heads under one hood. So be it! So be it! But how about giving me back my bird's nest? You have no more need of it now and are far too honorable a gentleman to want to withhold something that does not by rights belong to you—and of course I expect no gratitude, I assure you, for I'd have been more than happy to lend it to you." Without batting an eye, he took the nest out of my hand, stuffed it into his pocket, and laughed at me again, indeed so loudly that the forest warden looked up at the sound. I sat there riveted to the spot.

"You must after all admit," he continued, "that a hood like this one is far more convenient. For it hides not only the man but his shadow as well, and as many other shadows as he cares to take under his wing. You will notice," he said, "that today I once again have two shadows on the leash." He laughed again. "Remember this, Schlemihl—what at first you refuse to do of your own free will you will be forced to agree to in the end. Why not buy the thing back and retrieve your bride—there's still time, I assure you—and together we'll see that Rascal swinging on the gallows where he belongs, that'd be an easy matter as long as there's rope enough to hold him. And I'll tell you what, I'll throw in my magic hood as part of the deal."

The old mother followed her husband out of the house, and the conversation began. "How is Mina?"

"She's crying."

"Oh, that foolish child! What's done is done!"

"I know, but to give her so soon to another—Father, how can you be so cruel to your own child!"

"No, Mother, you've got the wrong idea. If before having wept her last childish tear she finds herself wed to a rich and honorable man, why, she'll wake relieved out of her misery as out of a bad dream, and she'll thank God and her parents for it, mark my word!"

"God willing!"

"She may now possess considerable assets, but after all the uproar of that unhappy affair with the adventurer has died down, do you really think she'd ever be likely to find so soon as good a match as Mr. Rascal? Do you have any idea how rich he is, this Mr. Rascal? He owns property hereabouts worth six million, no mortgages, all paid for in cash. I held the deeds in my own hands! It was he who beat me to the choice pickings everywhere; and in addition to that, he has IOUs from Mr. Thomas John for about four and a half million."

"He must have stolen a lot."

"How can you talk like that! He saved wisely where others tossed money to the wind."

"He was a livery servant by trade."

"Nonsense! Does he not possess an impeccable shadow?"

"Maybe you're right, but—"

The man in the gray coat laughed and looked at me. The door flew open, and out stepped Mina. She was leaning on the arm of a lady-in-waiting; quiet tears ran down her lovely pale cheeks. She lowered herself into a chair that had been set out for her under the linden trees, and her father pulled up a chair beside her. He gently took her hand in his, and spoke to her in a kindly voice as she burst into another fit of weeping.

"You are my good, sweet child, you'll be sensible, I'm sure, and won't disappoint your dear old father who has nothing but your happiness at heart. I understand, my dear, how deeply upset you are, but a lucky turn of events allowed you to elude your misfortune! I know, before we discovered his shameful charade, how much you loved that no-good cad; you see, Mina, I do not fault you for the depth of your feelings. I myself, dear child, was deceived by him, I loved him too, so long as I took him for a noble personage. But now you yourself must admit that everything has changed. For heaven's sake, every low-down dog has a shadow, and to think that my beloved only child should wed a man who—no, you must put him out of your mind at once. Listen, Mina, a gentleman has come to woo you, a man not afraid to be seen in broad daylight, an honorable man, who may not be a count, but he's worth ten million, ten times more than you own, a man who will make my beloved child happy. Don't contradict me now, don't oppose my will, just be my sweet, obedient daughter, and permit your loving father to fend for you, and dry those tears. Promise me that you will agree to marry Mr. Rascal. Now then, will you give me your word?"

She replied in a muffled murmur, "I have no more will of my own, no further wish on earth. Let my father do with me as he wants."

At that very moment, Rascal was announced and strode impudently into their midst. Mina collapsed in a faint. My hated companion gave me an angry look. "How could you let this happen! Is it blood or water you have running through your veins?" With a rapid motion, he scratched a surface wound in my hand, I bled, and he continued, "Red blood indeed! Now then, sign!" And he thrust the parchment and quill into my hands.

–7–

I will defer to your judgment, dear Chamisso, and not attempt to sway you with sweet lies. I myself have long weighed my guilt, nurturing the torturous worm of conscience in my heart. This solemn moment of my life kept hovering before me as if it were only yesterday, and I could only bear to look askance at it with contrition and humility. Dear friend, whosoever frivolously sets foot on the straight and narrow path intending to persevere, he will be lured unexpectedly down other byways that lead him downward and ever downward to his doom; to no avail are the guiding lights he may glimpse shimmering in the night sky, he has no choice but to keep right on walking into the abyss, to sacrifice himself to the ineluctable nemesis of his deeds. Following that impetuous error that brought this curse upon me, trifling with love, I callously ploughed into the destiny of another; and there where I had despoiled goodness, where only a quick move could save the day, what else could I do but leap blindly to the rescue? For the final hour had struck.

Don't think so badly of me, Adelbert, as to suppose that any price would have seemed too dear, that I would have skimped on anything in my possession, be it goods or gold. No, Adelbert; but my soul was filled with insurmountable loathing for that inscrutable creature who had led me down the crooked path. It may be that I did him an injustice, but I could not bear to have any further truck with him. And here again, as so often before in my life, and in the history of the world for that matter, happenstance took the place of action. Years later I finally made peace with myself. I first had to learn to respect necessity—what's done is done, what's happened has happened, the past is a fait accompli. And then I learned to respect this necessity in and of itself as the wise and providential force that holds sway over the whole grand scheme of things, the machinery in which we are but inconsequential cogs, driven and driving through no will of our own; what must be must be, and what had to happen happened, and all is governed by that providential force that I finally learned to honor as the master of my destiny and the destiny of those who crossed my path.

I don't know if I ought to ascribe it to the strain on my soul in the sway of such mighty emotions or to my state of total exhaustion, drained as I was by the unceasing travail of the past few days, or to the destructive agitation stirred up in my very nature by the proximity of that gray fiend—for whatever reason, I fell unconscious when the time came to sign, and for a long time I lay as if in death's embrace.

The sounds of stamping and cursing were the first to strike my ear as I came to again. I opened my eyes and it was dark; my hated companion was busy rebuking me. "Carrying on like an old woman! We had best pull ourselves together and make good our resolve, or have we had a change of heart and would rather lie here blubbering?" With great effort I sat up on the ground where I had lain and silently peered about. It was late evening, and festive music emanated from the lighted windows of the forest warden's house as small groups of celebrants strolled up and down the paths in the garden. One couple stepped closer and sat down on the bench on which I had previously been seated.

They spoke of the marriage that had taken place that very morning between the wealthy Mr. Rascal and the daughter of the household. So it had finally happened.

I brushed off my head the magic hood of invisibility the mysterious stranger had lain upon it, whereupon he immediately disappeared and I in turn hurried off in silence to bury myself in the dark wall of bushes. Making my way to Count Peter's bower, I approached his garden gate. Invisible all the while, my tormentor kept hounding me with sharp words. "So this is the thanks I get for all my efforts on your behalf, Monsieur, with your weak nerves, the thanks for nursing you the whole day long. And I thought we'd dropped the joker from our deck. Very well, Mr. Thickhead, you just go on trying to elude me, don't you know we're inseparable, as thick as two thieves? You have my gold and I have your shadow; that tightens the bond between us. Has anyone ever heard of a shadow forsaking its master? Yours keeps me tied to you, until you mercifully take it back and rid me of its burden. What you failed to do of your own free will you'll have to do anyway—too late alas—in disgust and ennui; you can't escape your fate." He kept jabbering on and on in the same scornful tone. I fled, but for naught; forever present, he kept bending my ear about his gold and my shadow. I couldn't even hear myself think.

Slinking along down deserted streets, I made my way home. When at last I stood before it, staring at the once-familiar façade, it was scarcely recognizable; not a single light burned behind its shattered windows. The doors were shut, no servants stirred within. That awful voice laughed out loud beside me. "That's how the cookie crumbles, chum! If it's any consolation, you'll find your faithful Bendel within; they brought him home in such a state that I'm quite sure he hasn't set foot outside since." He laughed again. "The old duffer'll have a few stories to tell! Very well then! So long for now, see you soon!"

I rang and knocked repeatedly; at last a light went on. "Who's there?" Bendel inquired from within. When the good man heard my voice, he could scarcely control his emotions; the door flew open, and we ran weeping into each other's arms. I found him changed, weak and sickly, but then I too had turned gray.

He led me through the ravaged rooms to an inner chamber that had been spared the fury of the crowd. He brought me food and drink, we sat down, and again he burst out weeping. He told me that he had pursued and wrestled so long with the man in gray, whom he'd spotted in possession of my shadow, determined as he was to wrest it from him, that he lost all trace of me and finally collapsed in exhaustion. Afterward, unable as he was to find hide nor hair of me anywhere, he returned to look after my property, when a mob, on Rascal's instigation, stormed the door, smashed the windows, and raged and looted to their heart's content. This was how they repaid the kindness of their benefactor. My servants took flight. The local constabulary forthwith declared me persona non grata and gave me twenty-four hours to pack up and leave. Moreover, he filled me in on the details I did not know of Rascal's material acquisitions and precipitous matrimony. That cunning scoundrel, the instigator of all the misfortunes that had befallen me here, must have known my secret from the very beginning; it appears that, attracted by the lure of gold, he managed to ingratiate himself with me. At the start he acquired a duplicate key to the cabinet in which I kept all my gold, and drawing freely thereupon, built his considerable fortune, to which he is still slyly adding to this day.

All this Bendel told me amid abundant tears, whereupon he wept again out of joy, this time to see me again, to have me there; having himself long despaired of establishing my whereabouts, wherever fate may have led me, he was happy to see me calmly and resolutely enduring my misfortune. For such was the expression that despair had carved in my face. I saw my misery, giant and immovable, towering before me; I had shed all my tears, not another moan could that specter squeeze from my breast; bare-headed, I bore my sorrow with the coldness and equanimity of a man who has nothing left to lose.

"Bendel," I said, "you know what lies in store for me. For the debts I amassed so blithely I must now pay a bitter interest. You are an innocent man, and must no longer bind your fate to mine; I cannot permit it. This very night will I ride off. Saddle my horse, for I ride alone; you must stay here, I insist. Surely there are still a few chests of gold lying about—they're yours. I will henceforth follow my restless path alone; but should I ever again be graced with a glimmering of joy, and fortune smile on me once more, then will I think of you again, for I wept on your breast in this, my heaviest, bitterest hour."

With a broken heart, that faithful honest man had to do his master's bidding this one last time, though his very soul shuddered at such a request. I turned a deaf ear to his pleading, I was blind to his tears, and he brought me the horse I asked for. One last time did I press his tear-filled face to my breast; then I swung myself up into the saddle and fled in the cloak of darkness from the grave of my life, little caring which direction my horse might choose; for I had no further destination on this earth, no wish, no hope.

-8-

A man on foot soon joined me. After he had walked a while beside my horse, he asked, seeing that we were headed in the same direction, if he might not rest his heavy coat on my horse's rear flanks; I acceded without a word. He thanked me for the kindness, praised my horse, took the opportunity to laud the fortune and power of the rich, and so launched into a kind of conversation with himself for which I served as a mere listening ear.

He elaborated his views on life and matters of wordly consequence, and soon came to the subject of metaphysics, challenging himself to find the key to all mysteries. He expounded with great clarity, and hastened to venture a reply to himself: You know, my friend, that though I once fancied myself a student of ideas, I have long acknowledged a lack of aptitude for philosophical speculation, and abandoned the field; since then I have let many matters rest, foresworn trying to know and understand everything, trusting instead, on your sound advice, my own instincts, the voice within, and have, insofar as I was able, followed my own path.

So it seemed to me that this able and articulate rhetorician skillfully built a solid, self-sustaining argument supported by its own inner necessity. Yet I found it altogether lacking in the very substance I would have liked to find, and thus I took it as a bit of mere artifice whose elegant closure and conclusiveness offered nothing but empty delight to the mind's eye; but I was glad nonetheless to listen intently, for my eloquent companion took my mind off my own misery, and I would just as willingly have given way had he attempted to lay claim to my soul as to my reason.

Meanwhile, time had rushed forward, and without my noticing it, dawn had already begun to brighten the night sky. I fell into a panic, when all at once I looked up and saw in the east the burst of color heralding imminent sunrise, and now, at the hour when the first shadows fall in all their ostentatious splendor, there was no protection, no refuge in sight on the open plain! And I was not alone! I looked back at my companion, and once again shuddered in fright. It was none other than the man in the gray coat.

He chuckled in amusement at my dumbfounded expression, and continued without letting me get a word in edgewise. "Come now, let our mutual benefit unite us for a while, as is only customary in this world; there's always time to part ways. This road skirting the mountain, in case you didn't realize it right away, is the only one you could possibly take; you dare not descend into the valley, much less turn back across the mountain to where you came from—and it just happens to be my road too. You're already blanching with horror at the prospect of the sunrise. Let me lend you back your shadow for the duration of our journey together, and all you need do in exchange is countenance my company. You no longer have your faithful Bendel; let me serve you in his stead. You don't like me, I know, and that makes me sad. My help may nevertheless still come in handy. The devil is not as black as they like to paint him. True, you annoyed me yesterday, but I won't hold it against you today, and I have after all made the road seem shorter, this you must admit. Why don't you just try your shadow back on for size?"

The sun had risen, people were approaching us on the road; I accepted his proposition, albeit reluctantly. Grinning, he let my shadow unravel and fall to the ground, and it immediately took its place beside the horse's shadow, both of them trotting merrily along. How strange I felt. I rode past a party of country bumpkins, who doffed their hats and humbly made way for a man of means. I rode on, peering down with a greedy eye and a beating heart at the shadow, formerly mine, which I had just borrowed back from a stranger, indeed from my mortal enemy.

Bemused, indifferent to my chagrin, he strode beside me, absentmindedly whistling a little tune. He on foot, I on horseback, the giddiness of the idea went to my head, the temptation was too great, all of a sudden I seized the reins, dug in with my spurs, and made a mad dash for it; the shadow, however, refused to follow, but pivoted free of the horse and paused, awaiting the arrival of its rightful owner. Red-faced with shame, I was obliged to turn back, while the man in the gray coat calmly finished whistling his little ditty and, laughing at me, reattached the shadow and warned that it would stick to my feet and stay with me only when I could again lay claim to it as my rightful possession. "I've got you by your shadow," he continued, "no sense trying to escape. A rich man like you needs a respectable shadow, there's no getting around it; it's just too bad you didn't see reason long ago."

I continued my journey along the same road; once again I enjoyed the amenities of life, delighting in the simple fact of existence; I was free to move about as I pleased, since I possessed, if but on temporary loan, a bona-fide shadow, and everywhere my appearance instilled the respect that wealth accords; and yet I carried death in my heart. My strange companion, who pretended to be the lowly servant of the richest man on earth, proved exceptionally adept at obsequious behavior; he was the very epitome of a rich man's lackey. But he never left my side, kept heaping scorn upon me, foreseeing with complete confidence the day when I would finally, if only to be rid of him, clinch the deal and offer my soul in exchange for my shadow.

His company was as burdensome to me as it was loathsome. I had good reason to fear him, for I had made myself dependent on him. After leading me back to the splendor of the world from which I had fled, he held me once again in his grip. I was obliged to endure his never-ending verbal assault, and I very nearly became convinced that he was right. A rich man must have a shadow in this world, and as soon as I sought to lay claim to the social standing to which, lured back by the devil, I once again aspired, I had only one option. And yet I stood firm in my resolve: having sacrificed my love, now that life itself had paled, I would not sell my soul to this creature for all the shadows in the world. But how was all this to end?

We were sitting upon an overlook to which all the travelers passing across these mountains pay a visit. You can hear the surging of underground streams bubbling up from immeasurable depths, and a stone tossed over the edge falls and falls without, it seems, ever striking the bottom. With a dizzying imaginative prowess and the shimmering dazzle of all the colors in his palette, my companion depicted for me, as was often his wont, in painstaking detail all the pleasures I would enjoy with the aid of my purse, if only I once again had possession of my shadow. My elbows propped upon my knees, I buried my face in my hands and listened to that false deceiver, my heart divided between the desire to succumb and the force of my willpower. I had come to the end of my rope, no longer able to endure such inner turmoil, and so I began the decisive final struggle: "You appear to forget, sir, that though I may have permitted you under certain circumstances to remain in my company, I retained the right of complete freedom of movement."

"Say the word and I'll be gone." This threat was often repeated. I remained silent; he immediately proceeded to roll up my shadow. I turned pale, but I let it happen without a word. A long silence followed. He was the first to break it.

"You cannot abide me, sir; you hate me, I know; but why do you hate me? Is it perhaps because you assaulted me on the open road with the intent of robbing me of my bird's nest? Or is it because you scurrilously attempted to make off with my possession, the shadow that you naively believed was entrusted to you on your honor? I for my part do not hate you for this; I find it perfectly natural that you should attempt to play all your cards, including deception and force; the fact that you nevertheless flatter yourself with having the strictest principles and believe yourself to be the epitome of honesty itself is a fancy to which I likewise have no objection. My morals may not be as strict as yours, but my actions match your principles to a T. Or did I ever press a thumb against your throat to take by force your worthy soul, for which I happen to have a hankering? Did I ever set a servant on you to reclaim the purse I traded in a fair exchange? Did I ever try to bolt with it?" I could offer no denial; he continued, "Very well, my good man, very well! So you can't abide my company; this too I understand, and do not hold it against you. We must go our separate ways, that much is clear, and you too are beginning to try my patience. So as to be rid once and for all of my shameful presence, let me recommend again: Buy the thing back from me!"

I held forth the purse. "Take this in exchange."

"No!"

I heaved a heavy sigh and spoke up again. "So be it. I demand it, sir: let us part immediately, cross my path no longer in a world which I trust is big enough for the two of us."

He smiled and replied, "I'll be gone, sir, but let me first instruct you how you may ring for me if ever you should desire the aid of your most humble servant. You have only to shake your purse so that the limitless store of gold coins rattles within; that sweet sound will immediately call me forth. Everyone thinks only of his own advantage in this world, but you see that I am also concerned with yours, for I am revealing to you a new strength at your disposal. Oh, that magic purse! For even had the moths already chewed up your shadow, this purse would still remain a strong bond between us. Enough, you're bound to me by the tinkle of my gold; your most humble servant will do your bidding from afar. You well know how useful I can be to my friends, and that the rich are particularly close to me; you have seen it yourself. But one thing, my good sir—this you must remember—you'll never get your shadow back except under one condition."

Faces from the past were suddenly recalled by my mind's eye. I asked him quickly, "Did you ever get a signature from Mr. John?"

He smiled. "Formalities were hardly needed with such a good friend."

"Where is he? By God, I want to know!" With some hesitation, he put a hand in his pocket, and plucked up by his hair there dangled the pale distorted figure of Thomas John, whose corpse-blue lips opened and closed, pronouncing the solemn words: "Justo judicio Dei judicatus sum; justo judicio Dei condemnatus sum."

Horrified, I heaved that rattling purse into the bottomless abyss and spoke these last words to him: "Accursed be you, Lucifer, in the name of God! Get thee hence and let me never more lay eyes on you!" Darkly scowling, he arose and immediately disappeared behind the wall of stone that bordered this overgrown spot.

–9–

I sat there without shadow or money, but a heavy weight had been lifted from my heart: I felt giddy. Had I not also lost my love, or were I to have felt myself blameless for that loss, I believe I could have been happy—but I had no idea what to do next. I searched my pockets and found a few remaining gold pieces; I counted them, and laughed. I had left my horse back at the inn. I was ashamed to return there, at least until the sun had set; it still hung high overhead. I lay down in the shadow of the nearest grove and fell fast asleep.

A swirl of enticing images coalesced into a sweet dream. Mina, wearing a wreath of flowers in her hair, brushed past me and flashed me a friendly smile. Even old faithful Bendel, bedecked with flowers, rushed by with a kind word of greeting. Many a familiar face did I see, including yours, dear Chamisso, if I'm not mistaken, among the gathering throng; a bright light shone, but no one cast a shadow, and what was stranger still, the spectacle was pleasing to the eye. Flowers and songs, love and happiness thrived in a palm grove; I could neither grasp nor make out clearly those light and lovable figures blowing past me like leaves, but I know that I was happy to be dreaming such a dream and I dreaded waking. And then, when I really was awake, I still kept my eyes closed to prevent the fleeting images from vanishing in the garden of my soul.

Finally I opened my eyes. The sun still hung in the sky, but in the east; I had slept through the night. I took it for a sign that I ought not return to the inn. It was easy to part with the last of my possessions, and I resolved to set out on foot along a back road that led through a wooded valley surrounding the mountain to fulfill whatever destiny held in store for me. I did not look back, and did not even think of turning to Bendel—whom I'd left a rich man—as well I might have. I looked myself over, this new persona that I was to assume in the world: my clothes were rather shabby. I had on an old black *kurtka,* which I had already worn in Berlin, and which for some reason I had dug up again at the start of this trip. In addition, I wore a traveler's cap on my head and a pair of old boots on my weary feet. I stood up, looked around, found and cut myself a walking stick as a kind of souvenir, and immediately continued on my journey.

In the forest I met an old peasant who offered me a friendly greeting and with whom I entered into conversation. Like a curious traveler, I inquired first concerning the state of the road, and then the region and its inhabitants, what minerals the mountain yielded, and the like. The man proved knowledgeable and well-spoken in his replies to my questions. We came to the bed of a mountain stream that had eroded a wide and winding gap through the forest. Shuddering inwardly at the prospect of crossing that sunny space, I let my companion go on ahead. But in the midst of that perilous terrain, he turned around to tell me the history of the erosion. It wasn't long before he noticed what I had missing, and he paused in mid-sentence: "But how can it be? The gentleman has no shadow!"

"Alas! Alas!" I replied with expressive sighs. "It was a long and terrible illness that robbed me of my hair, fingernails, and shadow. See, little father, at my young age, the hair that grew back is completely white, the nails very short, and the shadow hasn't grown back yet."

"Oh no! Oh no!" the old man muttered, shaking his head, "it's an awful thing to be without a shadow, that must have been one hell of an illness the gentleman had!" He did not, however, resume his account of the erosion, and at the next fork in the road he ran off and left me without a word of farewell. Once again a flood of bitter tears cascaded down my cheeks, and my new-found happiness was dashed to pieces.

With a sad heart, I continued on my way and sought no further human contact. I stuck to the darkest woods, and sometimes had to wait hours before crossing a strip of land on which the sun shone so that no human eye might bar my passage. Evenings I sought refuge in the scattered villages. My actual destination was a mine in the mountain in which I planned to seek work underground; for notwithstanding that my present condition compelled me to fend for myself, I realized full well that only strenuous physical labor could protect me from my own dark thoughts.

A few rainy days enabled me to make good headway, but at the cost of my boots, the soles of which were designed for Count Peter and not for an itinerant wanderer. They were already worn clear through to my bare feet. I absolutely needed a new pair of boots. The next morning I set about this business with zeal, scouting the stalls at a country fair until I found one that sold boots new and used. I picked and haggled for the longest time. I was obliged to renounce a brand-new pair that caught my eye and that I would very much have liked to acquire, but the price was well beyond my means. I made do instead with a pair of second-hand boots that still seemed strong and solid, and that the genial blond lad who ran the stall handed over with a smile in exchange for cash, wishing me well on my way. I put them on immediately and headed north.

I was very much lost in thought, and hardly noticed where I set my feet; my mind was on the mine, which I still hoped to reach that evening, but at which I did not rightly know how I was going to present myself. I had scarcely walked two hundred paces when I noticed that I had wandered off the beaten track; I looked around in search of the trail and realized that I stood in the midst of a vast and ancient forest of virgin evergreens never grazed, so it seemed, by the blade of the ax. Proceeding another few paces, I found myself surrounded by barren cliffs on which only moss and saxifrage grew, and the gaps in between were covered with fields of snow and ice. The air was exceedingly cold; I looked around and noticed that the forest had disappeared behind me. Another few paces—around me loomed a deathlike silence; the sheet of ice on which I stood, and over which a thick fog hung, seemed to stretch for miles around me; the sun dangled bloody on the edge of the horizon. The cold was unbearable. I had no idea how I had got here; the numbing frost compelled me to hasten my steps; the only sound I heard was the rush of distant waters. Another step, and I landed at the icy edge of an ocean. Countless herds of seals leaped noisily before me into the tide. I followed the shoreline and saw once again in the distance naked cliffs, dry land, birch and evergreen forests, then I ran on for a few minutes dead ahead. It was suffocatingly hot; I looked around. To one side stretched cultivated rice fields and to the other mulberry trees. I sat down in the shadow of the latter and peered at my watch; not a quarter of an hour had passed since I'd left the marketplace.

I thought I must be dreaming, and bit my tongue to wake myself, but I actually was awake. I closed my eyes in order to collect my thoughts. Then I heard curious nasal syllables being uttered nearby and looked up: two Chinamen, unmistakable in their Asiatic features (even if I were to doubt the authenticity of their costume) addressed me in what I imagine must have been the common local greeting. I got up and stepped back two paces. The Chinamen were gone, the landscape was altogether different: trees and forests stretched before me instead of rice fields. I studied the trees and other flora that blossomed around me: those I recognized were of a Southeast Asian species. Intending to approach one tree for a closer look, I took a step forward—and once again, eveything had changed. So I continued walking like a recruit in training, proceeding slowly but with a dogged determination. Wondrously changing vistas, flora, fields, mountains, tundras, and sandy deserts unfurled themselves before my marveling gaze. There was no doubt about it: I had seven-league boots on my feet.

10

I fell to my knees in silent devotion and wept tears of thanks —for all at once my future revealed itself to me. Cast out from human society because of my early trespasses, I had been sent back to nature, the realm I have always cherished; the earth had been given me as a fertile garden to tend, the study of which was henceforth to be the direction and motivating force of my life, a life wholly devoted to science. This was not so much a resolve as a vision. For ever since that moment I have sought faithfully, with a quiet, firm, unceasing zeal to realize and render the original image that came to my inner eye complete in a bright and crystal-clear flash; and henceforth my sense of self-worth will forever depend ineluctably on my ability to make the rendering true to the original vision.

I pulled myself together, and without a moment's hesitation took a quick look around, laying instant claim to the field I would henceforth be harvesting. I stood on the mountain tops of Tibet, and the sun that had just risen before my eyes a few hours ago was already sinking into the firmament of the night sky; I strode through Asia from east to west, keeping a step ahead of the sun in its rapid descent, and crossed over into Africa. I looked around eagerly, scanning the entire continent in all directions. As I gaped at the old pyramids and temples of Egypt, I happened to spy in the desert, not far from Thebes with its hundred gates, those caves inhabited in former times by Christian anchorites.

All at once I knew that this was to be my home. I selected as my future domicile one of the most remote, albeit spacious and comfortable, caves, a lair inaccessible to jackals, and then I continued on my way. At the Pillars of Hercules, I crossed over into Europe, and after inspecting its southern- and northernmost provinces, I stepped from Northern Asia via the North Pole from Greenland into America, wandered through both the northern and southern half of that continent, and encountering the onset of winter in the south, turned in my tracks and headed back northward across Cape Horn.

I lingered until day broke in the Far East, and only after a good long rest did I resume my wanderings. I followed the mountain chain with the highest known elevations on earth through both Americas. Slowly and carefully I stepped from peak to peak, sometimes over flaming volcanos, sometimes over snow-covered domes, often pausing to catch my breath; at last I reached Mount Elias and leaped across the Bering Straits back into Asia. I followed the west coast of that continent along its many twists and turns and took pains to explore those islands accessible to me. From the Malacca Peninsula my boots carried me across to Sumatra, Java, Bali, and Lamboc; I attempted repeatedly, at considerable risk, though always unsuccessfully, to ford across to the smaller islands and promontories that speckle the sea in those parts, and thereby to facilitate a northwest passage to Borneo and the other outlying islands of the archipelago. I was obliged to abandon the effort. At the tip of Lamboc I finally sat down with my face turned to the south and to the east and I wept, rattling, as it were, the gates of my far-flung prison, for here at last I was forced to acknowledge my limitations. New Holland, that remarkable place, and the South Sea islands, whose sun-bathed cloak of flora and fauna are so essential to a complete picture of the earth's life forms, would be forever off-limits to me; and thus, in essence, all that I could possibly collect and comment upon was doomed to remain a mere fragment of the whole. Oh, dear Adelbert, what are man's efforts on this earth but vain illusions!

Often in the dread winter of the southern hemisphere I have tried to push westward across the North Pole and tackle those two hundred paces separating Cape Horn from Van Diemen's Land and New Holland, with no care for how I might return, daring the ice cap to close in upon me like a coffin lid, stepping with wild abandon from iceberg to iceberg, oblivious to the gaping jaws of the frozen deep. And all for naught; New Holland still eludes me. Each time I returned to Lamboc and sat down on its tip, and wept again with my face turned to the south and to the east, rattling the gates of my prison.

I finally lifted myself up by my bootstraps, as it were, and strode with a heavy heart back into the interior of Asia. I traversed it then, ever following the dawn breaking in the west, and that same night arrived in Thebes at the entrance to the cave I'd selected just the afternoon of the day before.

As soon as I was somewhat rested and day broke over Europe, I made it my first order of business to go about acquiring the necessities of life. First off, I needed a pair of brake-shoes; for I had learned just how uncomfortable it could be to have no means of curtailing my step (other than to remove my boots) if, say, I wanted to take a closer look at some nearby object. A pair of bedroom slippers slipped on over the boots filled the bill, just as I hoped they would, and later I took to carrying two pairs with me, for I was often obliged to kick off the ones I had on without time enough to retrieve them whenever, in the course of my botanical exploits, lions, humans, or hyenas took me by surprise. My fine timepiece served me well as an excellent chronometer on these short jaunts. In addition, I needed a sextant, a few geometric instruments, and books.

In order to procure the latter, I paid several uneasy visits to Paris and London, where I was shrouded by a fortuitous fog. Once the meager remains of my magical money had been spent, I offered payment in the form of easy-to-find specimens of African ivory, whereby I was naturally obliged to pick out the smaller portable teeth. Soon I had furnished and equipped myself with all that I needed, and I immediately commenced my new life as an independent naturalist.

I crisscrossed the globe, now gauging its altitudes, now measuring the temperature of its springs and of the air above, now observing fauna, now examining flora; I rushed from the Equator to the North Pole, from one region to another, comparing my impressions and experiences. The eggs of the African ostrich or the Northern seabird as well as fruits, particularly those of the tropical palm tree and bananas, served as my common fare. As a surrogate for happiness I had nicotine, and in place of human compassion and companionship I had the love of a faithful poodle who watched over my cave in the Theban hills, and when I returned home laden with new treasures, leaped at me for joy and consoled me with the human sense that I was not alone on this earth. But one more adventure was still to bring me back among humankind.

-11-

Once, when I wiled on shore of the frozen north, having braked my boots to collect lichen and algae, a polar bear suddenly stepped out from behind a boulder and caught me unawares. I intended, after tossing away my slippers, to step over to a nearby island to which a naked rock jutting up out of the ocean offered access. With one foot I landed firmly on the rock, and went tumbling on its far side into the sea, for unbeknownst to me the slipper had remained attached to my other boot.

The icy chill engulfed me, and struggling to stay afloat I barely managed to save my life; as soon as I reached dry land, I ran as quickly as I could toward the Libyan desert to dry off in the sun. But once exposed to the full force of its powerful rays, I was burned so badly on the top of my head that I hurried back northward in an acutely feverish state. I sought by means of vigorous exercise to improve my condition, and ran with a quick and shaky step from west to east and back again from east to west. Thus I stumbled from broad daylight into darkest night, from summer swelter into the icy dead of winter.

I have no idea how long I kept scurrying about in this fashion across the surface of the globe. A burning fever ran like lava in my veins; terrified, I felt myself fast losing consciousness. To add to my troubles, in the course of such careless globetrotting I happened to stamp on someone's foot. I must have hurt him badly, for I received a mighty shove and collapsed in a swoon.

When I came to again, I found myself comfortably ensconced in a fine bed that stood among other beds in a spacious and stately hall. Someone was seated at my feet; people wandered through the hall from one bed to the next. They came to my bed and discussed my case. They referred to me, however, as Number 12, even though I discovered on the wall at my feet a black marble tablet on which, clearly inscribed in gold letters—it was no illusion, I could read it clearly—there was my name

PETER SCHLEMIEL

spelled correctly. On the tablet beneath my name there were another two rows of letters, but I was far too weak to make any sense of them, and I shut my eyes again. I heard a voice reading aloud from a document concerning said Peter Schlemiel, but was unable to follow the words; I noticed a kindly-looking gentleman and a very beautiful lady in black approach my bed. The faces were not altogether strange to me, and yet I could not place them.

In a little while I regained consciousness. I was identified as Number 12, and because of his long beard, Number 12 was taken for a Jew, though he was not treated any the worse for it. The fact that he had no shadow appeared to have gone unnoticed. My boots, I was assured, along with everything else found on my person when they brought me here, were kept under lock and key and would be returned to me as soon as I was well enough to leave. The place where I lay sick was called the SCHLEMILIUM; the text concerning Peter Schlemiel read aloud from daily was an exhortation to pray for his welfare as the founder and benefactor of this charitable institution. The kindly gentleman was none other than Bendel, the lovely lady was Mina.

I lay there convalescing incognito, and learned more interesting facts: the locale was Bendel's native town; here, with what was left of my accursed gold, he had founded and taken over the direction of this hospital in my memory, where poor unfortunates hallowed my name. Mina was a widow; criminal proceedings had cost Mr. Rascal his life and her the remains of her fortune. Her parents were deceased. She lived here as a God-fearing widow practicing daily acts of charity.

On one occasion I happened to overhear the following conversation between her and Mr. Bendel at the bedside of Number 12: "But why, kind lady, must you continuously expose yourself to the evil humors of this place? Has fate been so hard on you that you wish to die?"

"Not at all, Mr. Bendel, ever since I dreamed that long-drawn-out dream of mine to the end and reawakened to myself, I've been quite well; since then I no longer wish for and no longer fear death. I now think pleasantly of the past and the future. Is it not also with the same quiet inner contentment that you now serve your old master and friend in such a blessed manner?"

"Yes indeed, thank God, kind lady. We've been through strange and wondrous things; unwittingly we sipped our fill of joy and bitter woe from the cup of life. And now that it's empty, one might well be tempted to believe that all that was only a test, and that now, fortified with the wisdom of experience, we stand before the real beginning. This is the real beginning, and though we do not wish the return of past delusions, we are nevertheless happy to have lived it as it was. And I also now feel confident that wherever he is our old friend must be doing better than before."

"I feel it too," replied the lovely widow, and they walked on past my bed.

This conversation made a profound impression on me; yet I fell into a deep quandary over whether to reveal my true identity or depart unrecognized. Finally I made my decision. Requesting pencil and paper, I jotted down the following words: "Your old friend is indeed doing better than before, and if his life now be taken up with works of atonement, it is the atonement of a man reconciled with life."

Hereupon, having regained my strength and feeling much better, I asked to be allowed to get dressed. They fetched the key to the little cabinet beside my bed. In it I found all my possessions. I put on my clothes, and over my old black *kurtka* I slung the botanical pouch (in which, to my great jubilation, I found again all the flora I had gathered in the Northern Hemisphere), slipped into my boots, laid the note I'd written on my bed, and as soon as the door was open, was already well on my way to Thebes.

Once I set foot again on the coast of Syria and returned along the same path that had last led me from home, I spotted my poor Figaro come bounding at me. That formidable dog appears to have attempted to follow the trail of his master, who left him languishing at home for such a long while. I stood still and called to him. He leaped upon me, barking with a thousand stirring exclamations of his innocent unfettered joy. I took him in my arms, for the poor beast was naturally unable to keep up with my boots, and brought him back home with me.

There I found everything as I had left it, and little by little, as my strength returned, I went back to my former pursuits and resumed my old life; except that for an entire year I avoided exposing myself to the bitter effects of the polar chill.

And this, my dear Chamisso, is how I still live today. My boots do not wear thin at the soles, as that very learned work by the famous Tieckius, *De rebus gestis Pollicilli,* once gave me to fear they would. The durability of my fine footwear remains unimpeded; only my own strength is fading; and yet I may console myself with the fact that I have not used them idly but have employed them consistently for the pursuit of knowledge and progress. I have, insofar as my boots permitted, gained a deeper knowledge and learned more than any man before me of the earth, its formation, its precipices, its atmospheres in their constant flux, the manifestations of its magnetic force, its life forms, particularly the flora. I have recorded the conditions I observed as accurately as I could in as clear a fashion as possible in many works, and noted down my conclusions and views in a few cursory papers.

I charted the geography of the interior of Africa and that of the frozen polar ice caps, mapped out Asia from its center to its eastern coastline. My *Historia stirpium plantarum utriusque orbis* is a major, albeit fragmentary, contribution to the flora universalis terrae and an important link in my systema naturae. In my painstaking work, I believe that I have not only increased by a third the number of known species, but have added my share to our knowledge of the natural order and the geography of plants. I am working studiously on my fauna. I will take pains to see that before my death my manuscripts are deposited in the library of the University of Berlin. And you, my dear Chamisso, I have chosen as the executor of my wondrous story, so that once I no longer walk the earth my story may yet serve as a moral lesson to some of its citizens. But to you, my dear friend, I say that if you wish to live among your fellow man, learn to value your shadow more than gold. If, on the other hand, you choose to live only for the sake of your own better self, then you need no advice from me.

EXPLICIT